LENDING POLICY
IF YOU DAMAGE OR LOSE THIS BOOK YOU
WILL BE CHARGED FOR ITS REPLACEMENT.
FAILURE TO PAY AFFECTS REGISTRATION,
TRANSCRIPTS, AND LIBRARY PRIVILEGES.

DISCARD

S0-ATA-136

At Issue

Are Americans Overmedicated?

Other Books in the At Issue series:

At Issue

Are Americans Overmedicated?

Amanda Hiber, Book Editor

GREENHAVEN PRESS
An imprint of Thomson Gale, a part of The Thomson Corporation

Detroit • New York • San Francisco • New Haven, Conn. • Waterville, Maine • London

Christine Nasso, *Publisher*
Elizabeth Des Chenes, *Managing Editor*

© 2006 Thomson Gale, a part of The Thomson Corporation.

Thomson and Star logo are trademarks and Gale and Greenhaven Press are registered trademarks used herein under license.

For more information, contact:
Greenhaven Press
27500 Drake Rd.
Farmington Hills, MI 48331-3535
Or you can visit our Internet site at http://www.gale.com

ALL RIGHTS RESERVED
No part of this work covered by the copyright hereon may be reproduced or used in any form or by any means—graphic, electronic, or mechanical, including photocopying, recording, taping, Web distribution, or information storage retrieval systems—without the written permission of the publisher.

Articles in Greenhaven Press anthologies are often edited for length to meet page requirements. In addition, original titles of these works are changed to clearly present the main thesis and to explicitly indicate the author's opinion. Every effort is made to ensure that Greenhaven Press accurately reflects the original intent of the authors. Every effort has been made to trace the owners of copyrighted material.

Cover photographs reproduced by permission of Brand X Pictures.

LIBRARY OF CONGRESS CATALOGING-IN-PUBLICATION DATA

Are Americans Overmedicated? / Amanda Hiber, book editor.
    p. cm. -- (At issue)
Includes bibliographical references and index.
ISBN-13: 978-0-7377-3401-0 (lib. hardcover : alk. paper)
ISBN-10: 0-7377-3401-9 (lib. hardcover : alk. paper)
ISBN-13: 978-0-7377-3402-7 (pbk. : alk. paper)
ISBN-10: 0-7377-3402-7 (pbk. : alk. paper)
  1. Drugs--United States--Juvenile literature. 2. Medication errors--United States--Juvenile Literature. I. Hiber, Amanda. II. Series: At issue (San Diego, Calif.)
  RM301.17.A74 2007
  362.29--dc22

                                        2006020093

Printed in the United States of America
10 9 8 7 6 5 4 3 2 1

Contents

Introduction

Since the "Me Decade" of the 1980s, some cultural critics have charged that American society is fixated on instant gratification. In a 2003 article in the *Christian Science Monitor*, law professor and author Jules Lobel writes, "Americans . . . today . . . gorge on fast food, sound bites, and one-liners. They breathe, move, think, and take in everything amid a culture of fast and faster." Fast food allows Americans to get and eat food quickly, the Internet provides constant instant access to all sorts of information, and cell phones allow people to reach each other almost anytime. Some argue that such short-term thinking has pervaded all aspects of American culture, including the way Americans think about their health care. Many Americans, these critics assert, are too apt to reach for a pill or other medication as a quick fix for their problems—many of which may not even be legitimate medical problems. Others disagree that Americans are overmedicated and argue that new medications are helping millions of people to overcome pain and lead healthier, happier lives.

In the past few decades pharmaceutical companies have developed hundreds of new prescription medications to treat a variety of conditions. Some experts believe that this proliferation of new drugs has encouraged Americans to rely on pills to solve their health problems rather than to take a long-term approach that includes lifestyle and behavioral changes. For example, when the antidepressant drug Prozac appeared on the market in 1987, followed by several others, millions of Americans turned to such medications instead of psychotherapy. In an article for the *New York Times*, journalist Erica Goode explains Prozac's initial success: "Getting Prozac did not even require seeing a mental health professional. General practitioners wrote—and continue to write—the majority of prescriptions. The drugs gradually became an option for the mildly depressed, the bereaved, the stressed and the rejected." Many critics of antidepressants have similarly argued that the medications have become a quick fix for patients who would be better off undergoing therapy to uncover and address the source of their depression, anxiety, or other emotional difficulties.

In response to these criticisms, supporters of the pharmaceutical industry argue that prescription medications are created with the intention of treating conditions that lifestyle changes alone cannot completely fix. They also believe that medications are most effective when patients who take them also make lifestyle changes to support their health. People with high cholesterol, for instance, can take cholesterol-lowering drugs but should also develop healthy habits such as eating a low-fat diet and getting regular exercise.

Proponents of prescription drugs also assert that for financial reasons the use of medication is often preferable to other, more invasive treatments such as surgery. "Increased spending on pharmaceuticals often leads to lower spending on other forms of more costly health care," says Marjorie Powell, senior assistant general counsel of the Pharmaceutical Researchers and Manufacturers of America (PhRMA). In this age of concern over soaring health care costs, affordable prescription medications that treat illnesses quickly and effectively are a welcome alternative to more expensive treatments.

A second major criticism of the pharmaceutical industry is that it is developing many medications for conditions that were once viewed and accepted as the normal inconveniences of everyday life. In a 2001 study of pharmaceutical advertising in popular magazines, Steven Woloshin and Lisa M. Schwartz of Dartmouth Medical School conclude,

> Our findings suggest that most prescription drugs advertised to consumers target common symptoms (e.g., sneezing, hair loss, being overweight), which many patients would have

managed without a physician. Although a pharmacological approach might be appropriate for some, the danger is that by turning ordinary experiences into diagnoses—by designating a runny nose as allergic rhinitis—the boundaries of medicine might become unreasonably broad. Some are concerned that Americans are growing more and more intolerant of the commonplace discomforts and imperfections of daily life and are overusing medications in their strivings for a utopian existence.

In defense of prescription drugs, some experts point out that this social critique ignores the reality of patients' suffering from conditions such as depression that have long been unrecognized or underdiagnosed. If the pharmaceutical industry has discovered effective treatments for these conditions that allow those who suffer from them to live better lives, they should be used, proponents argue. As Paul Antony, chief medical officer of PhRMA, writes:

> Prior to the 1990s, it was estimated that about half of those persons who met a clinical definition of depression were not appropriately diagnosed, and many of those diagnosed did not receive clinically appropriate treatment. However, in the 1990's, with the advent of SSRIs [selective serotonin reuptake inhibitors, the class of antidepressants that includes Prozac], treatment has been expanded. Antony and others believe that people should not have to suffer unnecessarily and should not be deterred from using medications that could help relieve their pain.

On the one hand, pharmaceutical innovation has saved and improved the lives of millions. However, like all technology that seeks to make life more comfortable and less painful, this innovation does carry risks, including dangerous side effects and adverse drug interactions. In *At Issue: Are Americans Overmedicated?* the authors debate whether Americans have become excessive in their use of medications, including treatments for depression, obesity, attention deficit disorder, chronic pain, and other disabling conditions. Given the vital importance of health and health care, having a greater understanding of these debates is crucial.

1

Americans Are Overmedicated

Katharine Greider

Katharine Greider is the author of The Big Fix: How the Pharmaceutical Industry Rips Off American Consumers. *Her articles, many of which focus on health and medical issues, have appeared in* Self, Mother Jones, *and other publications.*

More and more, patients' reported satisfaction with a doctor's visit is linked to whether or not they are given a prescription. Many see medication as the simple and obvious answer to any health problem, which can result in physicians feeling pressured to prescribe medications, even when they are not appropriate. The aging of the baby boomers, who promise to be much more proactive about their health care than were previous generations, is also leading to an increase in the use of prescription drugs. Indeed, taking several medications daily is becoming common among Americans. Many patients take one drug just to combat the side effects of another. Furthermore, the more medications a patient takes, the higher the likelihood of a dangerous drug interaction. Thousands of people die every year as a result of these fatal interactions.

It has been suggested that the impulse to use drugs is universal, a trait that distinguishes human beings from other animals. And isn't there something inherently appealing about taking medicine? You swallow it—you get better. Get-

Katharine Greider, *The Big Fix: How the Pharmaceutical Industry Rips Off American Consumers.* New York Public Affairs, 2003. Reproduced by permission of the author.

ting a medicine defines and validates one's suffering, while offering the promise of a solution. Indeed, though the term "drug hunger" most often describes the cravings of addiction, Jerry Avorn, MD, of Harvard Medical School, has applied it to the cold sufferer who won't be satisfied without a prescription for an antibiotic (even though the cold's likely cause is a virus that won't respond to antibiotics). "In a real sense," writes Avorn in *Annals of Internal Medicine*, "the drug prescription prolongs the physician-patient encounter by enabling the patient to ingest 'a dose of the doctor' several times a day." Ironically, doctors under pressure from insurers to manage costs have an incentive to get busy and write a script—an "office-visit-terminating event," as physician Ralph Gonzales quips.

It's becoming more common for individuals to take six, eight, or more prescriptions and over-the-counter medicines on a regular basis.

And the feeling they're getting the bum's rush may leave patients with an even greater desire for that take-away dose of attention. Gonzales, an expert in appropriate antibiotic use at the University of California, San Francisco, and author of *Practice Guidelines in Primary Care*, cites a study in which patients who felt they were treated with respect and care by a physician were satisfied without a prescription. But some of those who came away with a prescription were satisfied even if they didn't feel well-treated by the doc. Patients, like doctors, are busy and may perceive drugs, especially acute-care medicines like antibiotics, as the no-nonsense means to an end. "The public view antibiotics as very powerful medicine, the strongest medicine we have for infections," says Gonzales. "If there's even a remote chance that the antibiotic might help them, they want it. And they want it because they need to get back to work, or back to their usual activity level."

More Medicines Available

There's also an important—and, for many people, advantageous—movement under way toward the use of medications to manage chronic conditions. ... There are many more medicines available for these conditions. Partly as a result of research demonstrating the benefits of the new meds, guidelines for treating conditions like hypertension, high cholesterol, diabetes, and osteoporosis have been broadened. Add to these factors the aging population. As baby boomers pass middle age, the percentage of North Americans sixty-five and older is expected to climb from 12.5 percent in 2000 to 20.3 percent in 2030. These new old people promise to be a different, more "proactive" breed. "My grandmother didn't like to take drugs. They came about during her lifetime," says J. Lyle Bootman, Ph.D., dean of the College of Pharmacy at the University of Arizona. "Now it's a totally different attitude: you've got an ailment, take a pill, you want to feel good, take a pill, you want more hair, take a pill. ... The bottom line is, we're going to have increased consumption."

Or as Beth Greck, Pharm. D., a pharmacist in Ashland, North Carolina, puts it: "We're making more drugs for more things. Every time the heart failure guidelines come out, there's a new medication. So if somebody has heart failure and diabetes, all of a sudden there are your ten medications. We have evidence that these medicines work, so we have to give them. Then what happens is you start treating side effects with another medication."

Increased Consumption

Not only are more people taking drugs, but it's becoming more common for individuals to take six, eight, or more prescriptions and over-the-counter medicines on a regular basis. Even when they're all effective, safe, and indicated in themselves, together they may simply be too much—physically, practically, and perhaps financially. "Typically, if you're unmanaged and taking eight or more prescription drugs, there's virtually 100-percent probability of having a drug-drug interaction that will have a negative impact on your health," says Wayne K. Anderson, Ph.D., dean of the School of Pharmacy and Pharmaceutical Sciences at the University of Buffalo.

For each dollar we spend on medicines, we spend another dollar to treat new health problems caused by the medicines.

When David Morris, MD, retired from a long career in academic medicine a few years ago to work in a nursing home in Riverdale, New York, he was "amazed" to see how drugs were being distributed. "If you have gas or sneeze or have an itch, a medicine is dispensed," he says. Morris began reviewing residents' medications—it was typical for them to be on eleven different drugs—and (if the patient was amenable) winnowing them down. He was able to monitor patients on a daily basis, so if, for example, someone's blood pressure went up after stopping the meds, he could start the patient on them again. But Morris says in the great majority of cases, nothing happened. In fact, some patients were relieved of disturbances in balance, sleep, or appetite.

The Costs of Medication

Unrecognized drug side effects are particularly of concern in the elderly, who tend to take more drugs but metabolize them differently than the younger people usually represented in drug-company studies. Anderson tells the story of an eighty-year-old man who had osteoarthritis and was given a drug that made him nauseated. His doctor prescribed an anti-nauseant, which, after several months, produced a tremor. The man went to another doctor, who diagnosed Parkinson's disease and prescribed drugs to treat it, which increased the patient's nausea, resulting in an increase of anti-nausea drugs. Finally, a pharmacist had a conversation with the man's wife and recommended he be admitted to the hospital, where the drugs were carefully withdrawn. "He was discharged with a single prescription—Tylenol, for the osteoarthritis. Over the course of a year this man had become bedridden and now he was able to get back into life," says Anderson.

Discussions about the benefits and costs of various drugs often neglect the real-world consequences not only of known side effects but also of doctors' mistakes, patients' haphazard adherence to drug regimens, and unpredictable reactions. Most experts agree the toll is staggering. A 1998 analysis puts the annual death rate at 106,000, making adverse reactions to medication the fifth leading cause of death in the United States. Based on a conceptual model they developed, Bootman and a colleague estimate [that] the cost of medication-related problems rivals that of cancer, Alzheimer's disease, and diabetes. In fact, according to this research, for each dollar we spend on medicines, we spend another dollar to treat new health problems caused by the medicines. "It happened in my family," says Bootman. "It happened to my grandmother. She got dizzy, fell down on our kitchen floor, broke her hip. . . . It happens to people *all the time.*"

2

Americans Are Not Overmedicated

Pharmaceutical Research and Manufacturers of America

Pharmaceutical Research and Manufacturers of America (PhRMA) is a Washington, D.C.–based advocacy group representing the pharmaceutical industry.

The Minnesota Attorney General's 2003 report on the pharmaceutical industry alleges that Americans are using too many unnecessary medications. This statement overlooks abundant evidence that American patients are, in fact, underusing medications. Recent studies have found, for instance, that many patients who could benefit from cholesterol-lowering medicines do not take them. Asthma, congestive heart failure, and depression are also reportedly undertreated. In addition, the report falsely claims that the rise in health care costs is primarily due to the increase in prescription drug use. In fact, drug spending accounts for a minor segment of health care spending.

The MAGR [Minnesota Attorney General's Report, *Follow the Money: The Pharmaceutical Industry; The Other Drug Cartel*, September 30, 2003] claims (using data from a 2001 Kaiser Family Foundation Report) that "prescription drug expenditures are the fastest growing segment in health care,

Pharmaceutical Research and Manufacturers of America, "The Minnesota Attorney General's Report on Pharmaceuticals: Correcting the Record," October 31, 2003. Reproduced by permission.

approaching 18 percent of all health care expenditures." However, the 18 percent cited by MAGR is *wrong*. The Kaiser report only looked at annual percent increase, not total health care spending. According to the Kaiser report, the "annual percent change" in prescription drug expenditures from 1999 to 2000 was 18 percent. *This does not mean that prescription drugs account for approximately 18 percent of all health care expenditures.*

While prescription drug spending is increasing, it remains a very small portion of the health care dollar. According to the Centers for Medicare & Medicaid Services (CMS), of every health care dollar spent in the U.S., about 10 cents is spent on outpatient prescription drugs, including brand medicines, generic drugs, and pharmacy—not the "18 percent" that the MAGR suggests.

Moreover, this 10 cents encompasses far more than the cost of brand name ingredients. It also includes generic ingredients, pharmacy costs, prescription benefit manager costs, and wholesaler and distributor costs. The MAGR never makes this clear. Rather, it implies that all prescription drug costs are attributable to brand name manufacturers.

Furthermore, prescription medications are not responsible for recent double-digit health insurance premium increases. According to *Milliman USA*, HMO's [health maintenance organizations] monthly spending on presription medicines averaged $27.79—out of total monthly expenditures of $212.71 per person. Moreover, based on the *Milliman USA* data, PhRMA [Pharmaceutical Research and Manufacturers of America] calculates that if *HMOs' spending* on medicines had not increased at all between 1997 and 2002, HMO premiums still would have increased by 57.9 percent.

Other Health Care Expenditures

According to a [2002] report released by the American Association of Health Plans, drugs, medical devices and medical advances (including advances in diagnostics and treatment) *combined* accounted for 22 percent of the total increase in health care premiums between 2001 and 2002. (Factors other than drugs, medical devices and medical advances accounted for 78 percent, or nearly four-fifths, of premium increases during this period.) Moreover, the study noted that this estimate "does not reflect potential future savings from drugs, medical devices, and other medical advances. For example, savings in future years may include reduced hospitalization and consumption of other healthcare services."

Likewise, prescription medications account for only a small share of Medicaid's cost growth (before considering the offsetting savings they generate on other health services). In 2001, Medicaid spending for Rx [prescriptions] accounted for 11.6% of total expenditures, and from 1996 to 2000 Medicaid prescription drug increases (including brand name drugs, generic drugs, and pharmacy services combined) accounted for just one-fifth of the total increase in Medicaid spending. Four-fifths of the increase in Medicaid spending was accounted for by other health care services.

Underuse of prescription medications occurred in seven of nine conditions studied *with prescription medicines as the recommended treatment.*

Underuse of Medicines

The MAGR suggests that there is "unnecessary consumption" of pharmaceuticals driven by direct-to-consumer advertising. This claim ignores voluminous evidence that patients are underusing medicines, which results in serious illnesses and large health costs that could have been avoided.

The MAGR's error is evident in a recent analysis of the growing number of patients taking cholesterol-lowering medicines—a category of medicines that is advertised to consumers. The [2003] analysis, published in the *Journal of Managed Care Pharmacy*, began with the fact that the number of patients taking cholesterol-lowering medicines increased rapidly between 1997 and 1999. It then examined the health characteristics of patients taking these medicines, to determine whether the increased use occurred among patients who needed the medicines or patients who did not need the medicine. The study concluded that the increase in the number of patients taking these medicines over time "did not appear to be associated with a shift towards patients with less CV [cardiovascular] risk." However, "*a substantial portion of patients continue to remain untreated and undertreated . . .*" [according to an October 2002 report in the *American Journal of Managed Care*]. In fact, while NHLBI [National Heart, Lung, and Blood Institute] guidelines indicate that 36 million Americans should be treated with cholesterol-lowering medicines, "less than 45 percent of patients who qualify for therapy receive treatment," [as scholar M.B. Battorff argues]. According to NHLBI Director Dr. Claude Lenfant, if the ATP [Adult Treatment Panel] III recommendations were followed, heart disease "would no longer be the No. 1 killer." These findings about a category of medicines with rapidly growing use stand in stark contrast to MAGR's claim of unnecessary consumption of medicines.

Evidence of Undertreatment

The data demonstrating underuse of needed medicines do not rest on a single study. In fact, on June 26, 2003, *The New England Journal of Medicine* published, "The Quality of Health Care Delivered to Adults in the United States," a landmark study that comprehensively addresses the question of whether medical care, including prescription medicines, is typically overused. The study, which was conducted by RAND Health and funded by The Robert Wood Johnson Foundation, found that *nearly half of all adults in the United States fail to receive recommended health care.* According to results from the surveyed population, *underuse of prescription medications occurred in seven of nine conditions studied* with prescription medicines as the recommended treatment. The results of this landmark study, authored by one of America's leading independent think tanks and published in one of America's leading medical journals, were not cited in the MAGR, which instead claims that pharmaceuticals are overused.

Another recent [2003] article published in *The Journal of Managed Care Pharmacy*, "Analysis of Medication Use Patterns: Overuse of Antibiotics and Underuse of Prescription Drugs for Asthma, Depression and CHF [congestive heart failure]," which examined claims data from 3 of the 10 largest health plans in California to determine the appropriateness of prescription medication use based upon widely accepted treatment guidelines, found that "effective medication appears to be underused." Of the four therapeutic areas for study— asthma, congestive heart failure, depression, and common cold or upper respiratory tract infections—asthma, congestive heart failure, and depression were undertreated. The researchers concluded that "*the results are particularly surprising and disturbing when we take into account the fact that three of the conditions studied (asthma, CHF, and depression) are known to produce high costs to the healthcare system.*" Notably medicines to treat two of the three conditions found to be undertreated are DTC [direct-to-consumer] advertised. Nonetheless, MAGR attacks DTC as causing overuse of medicines, without ever discussing the costs or serious health consequences associated with the real issue—underuse of medicines to treat these illnesses.

Data from the National Committee on Quality Assurance (NCQA) adds to the voluminous data documenting underuse of medicines. NCQA, which includes representation of key health care purchasers and health plans on its governing board, publishes a broad array of quality measures covering the health care delivered to individuals with managed care insurance. A few of these measures cover use of medicines for treating chronic illnesses, such as asthma and depression. The results here, as in the studies above, demonstrate underuse of medicines.

3

Americans Are Overmedicated with Psychiatric Drugs

Fred Leavitt

Fred Leavitt holds a PhD in psychopharmacology from the University of Michigan. He has published several journal articles and textbooks and currently teaches psychology at California State University, Hayward.

Unlike other physicians, psychiatrists must seek out patients by persuading them that they need treatment. Drug companies are happy to assist them in this pursuit, as it ultimately boosts their sales. Thus, psychiatrists and drug companies work together to promote the connection between brain defects and mental disorders. Modern drugs are then offered as the solution for supposed chemical imbalances in the brain. However, there is substantial evidence that mental disorders are not caused by problems in the brain and that patients are being overprescribed psychiatric drugs when alternative treatments such as psychotherapy would be more effective.

Doctors in most medical specialties do not recruit patients. People know either directly or from diagnostic tests when they are ill. Psychiatrists, by contrast, must persuade troubled

Fred Leavitt, *The Real Drug Abusers*. Rowman & Littlefield, 2003. Copyright © 2003 by Rowman & Littlefield Publishers, Inc. Reproduced by permission.

people that they are sick and in need of professional help. For this they rely on drug companies. Drug companies help in three ways. First, they finance "educational" campaigns to persuade the public that sadness, shyness, boisterousness, anxiety, and other symptoms within the normal realm of human experience are actually diseases that require treatment with drugs. Second, they subsidize journals, conferences, and symposia. Between 20 and 30 percent of the American Psychiatric Association's operating budget comes from drug companies. Third, drug companies join with the psychiatric profession and the National Institute of Mental Health (the federal agency that funds much psychiatric research) to promote the view that brain defects are the primary cause of mental disorders. One observer asserted that "the pharmaceutical industry is a lobby within psychiatry, pushing for biological findings in etiological research [research seeking the causes of a disease] and thus justifying biological treatments." Their spokespeople argue that modern drugs correct chemical imbalances and should therefore be the treatment of choice. They portray the therapeutic effects of their products in terms of actions on specific neurotransmitters (NTs). For example, the effectiveness of the first generation of antipsychotic drugs mirrored their ability to block a subset of dopamine receptors. That led to the hypothesis that schizophrenia is caused by hyperactivity of brain dopaminergic systems. Similarly, antidepressant drugs target the presumed biological cause by enhancing the functioning of norepinephrine, serotonin, or both [dopamine, norepinephrine, and scrotonin are chemicals called neurotransmitters in the brain]. Antianxiety drugs increase the efficiency of gamma aminobutyric acid (GABA) synapses, which are presumed defective in anxiety disorders. [One researcher] writes, "There is no doubt that the development of drugs that interact with the brain-mind's chemical system is the most important advance in the history of modern psychiatry."

Dissenting Views

But scores of critics have expressed doubt. Whereas debates about drug industry profits typically feature adversaries who differ professionally and economically—company executives versus consumers—both advocates and dissenters on the issue of effectiveness of psychiatric drugs come from the ranks of therapists and researchers. Biopsychologist Elliot Valenstein has written, "Contrary to what is claimed, no biochemical, anatomical, or functional signs have been found that reliably distinguish the brains of mental patients"; he adds that "people with mental disorders may be encouraged when they are told that the prescribed drugs will do for them just what insulin does for a diabetic, but the analogy is certainly not justified."

Fred Baughman cites Surgeon General David Satcher: "Mental illness is no different than diabetes, asthma or other physical ailments. Mental illnesses are physical illnesses. We know the chemical disorders we are treating." Then Baughman responds:

> The presence of any bona fide disease, like diabetes, cancer, or epilepsy is confirmed by an objective finding—a physical or chemical abnormality. No demonstrable physical or chemical abnormality: no disease!... [T]here is no physical or chemical abnormality to be found, in life, or at autopsy in depression, bipolar disorder and other mental illnesses. Why, then, are you telling the American people that "mental illnesses" are "physical" and that they are due to "chemical disorders"?

Painful life experiences might be at the root of both [psychiatric] disorders and [brain] defects.

The theories relating schizophrenia to dopamine excess, and depression to insufficient norepinephrine or serotonin, originated when only a few NTs were known. Since then, researchers have identified many more—plus other features of neurotransmission that allow for enormous complexity and gradation of response. It is simplistic to reduce emotional state and cognitive functioning to the activity of single NTs. Recent evidence points to roles for the neuropeptide substance P. dopamine and acetylcholine in depression.

One reason for the disagreement between proponents and critics of psychiatric drugs is a turf war. Psychotherapists with degrees in psychology cannot prescribe drugs, whereas psychiatrists, with M.D.s, can. So the psychotherapists prefer environmental explanations of abnormality, and psychiatrists seek neuroanatomical and biochemical causes and cures.

No Proof of Cause

Even if it were shown unambiguously that victims of psychiatric disorders have brain defects, the finding would not prove that defects cause the disorders. Painful life experiences might be at the root of both the disorders and the defects. Trauma, stress, sexual abuse, neglect, and boredom not only cause emotional problems but can also change brain chemistry. People born after 1945 have a five- to twenty-fold higher lifetime prevalence rate of depression than those born before 1934. During those years, family structures, schooling, and other environmental factors changed considerably; inherited brain chemistry almost certainly did not.

Even staunch advocates of psychiatric drugs acknowledge that the vast majority relieve symptoms without curing.

Although mental illness increases the likelihood that a person will become homeless, many homeless people are merely victims of unfortunate circumstances. Yet society devalues them. The homeless are exposed to daily privation, dangers, powerful stressors, and loss of self-esteem. Such factors often precipitate the onset of mental health problems.

Previously healthy homeless people may start to behave outside the norm and be diagnosed as mentally ill.

Alternatives Ignored

In addition to the alliance between drug companies and psychiatrists, at least two other factors lead to overprescription of psychiatric drugs. First, most health maintenance organizations [HMOs] limit the number of sessions for which they reimburse therapists who treat psychiatric disorders. Talking therapies require frequent visits, whereas drugs, after the initial visit, can be prescribed by telephone. Thus, economic pressures force even those psychiatrists who would prefer to do psychotherapy into prescribing drugs. Psychiatrists must often evaluate a patient after a single session, and some HMOs relieve them of even that task. Psychiatrist Thomas Jensen filed suit against the Kaiser Permanente Medical Group in San Diego, claiming that it fired him after he refused to prescribe drugs to patients solely on the recommendations of social workers.

Second, primary care doctors are less likely to refer patients to psychiatrists than to other specialists. The primary care doctors prescribe drugs as their first line of treatment when various alternatives would often be preferable. As psychiatry is not their specialty, they have limited knowledge about the drugs and are especially susceptible to the tactics of detailmen [pharmaceutical company representatives who promote new drugs to physicians].

Even staunch advocates of psychiatric drugs acknowledge that the vast majority relieve symptoms without curing. Thus, patients must take the drugs for life or run a substantial risk of relapse. If the drugs were clearly better than alternatives, there would be no controversy. But they cause side effects (which are probably substantially underreported), cost money, and are often aversive to patients, so the burden of proof should be with the prescribers. Nevertheless, the psychopharmacological treatment of psychiatric disorders has become a multibillion-dollar business. Psychiatric drugs account for almost 11 percent of covered prescription drug costs and are the largest single drug-cost category for nearly half of pharmacy benefit management companies.

4

Americans Are Not Overmedicated with Psychiatric Drugs

Maia Szalavitz

Maia Szalavitz is a senior fellow at the media watchdog group STATS and author of the 2006 book Help at Any Cost.

There is no shortage of opponents to psychiatric drugs who claim that taking such drugs is simply a means of escaping problems rather than confronting them through talk therapy or other methods. Such critics seem to rely on the ancient notion that there is something noble in enduring pain. However, it is illogical to believe that it is acceptable for victims of physical trauma to take medication but that victims of emotional trauma should not receive similar help. Although critics of psychiatric drugs tend to overemphasize the negative side effects of medications, millions of Americans have been helped by these drugs. Furthermore, although some argue that psychotherapy is preferable to drug treatment, talk therapy, in fact, carries its own risks—in some cases, psychotherapy patients have been encouraged to dwell on their problems rather than solve them, and many patients have been sexually abused by their therapists. Psychiatric drugs help many people suffering from devastating conditions such as depression and anxiety to have a better quality of life.

Maia Szalavitz, "In Defense of Happy Pills," *Reason*, v. 37, October 2005. Copyright 2005 by Reason Foundation, 3415 S. Sepulveda Blvd., Suite 400, Los Angeles CA 90034, www.reason.com. Reproduced by permission.

Few would dispute the notion that painful experience can build character, just as stressing muscles by lifting weights increases strength. But it's also clear that most people most of the time prefer to avoid pain. The tension between these facts has led to a curious situation in mental health: Unlike in any other area of medicine, treatments that reduce pain and suffering, rather than being welcomed as miraculous breakthroughs, often are denigrated as "quick fixes." They're viewed as band-aids that cover up, but do not solve, the real problem—only marginally more acceptable than illicit drugs. "I oppose the use of heroin for the same reason I oppose the use of Prozac," the psychologist Jeffrey Schaler writes in his 2001 book *Addiction Is a Choice*. "I think relying on these is an existential cop-out—a way of avoiding coping with life."
. . .

Quick Fixes?

Anxieties about antidepressants, magnified by the ongoing debate over their side effects, extend beyond mental health professionals who face competitors with prescription pads. They also show up in the qualms of psychiatrists who worry that these drugs can be dangerous short cuts and in the public statements of regulators who suggest they're overused. Most important, the backlash against antidepressants may discourage people they would help from trying them by reinforcing the sense that there is something fundamentally suspect about turning to drugs for assistance in coping with life. Although the critics of drug therapy raise some valid points, the premise that pills are bad because they're easy is pernicious and needs to be challenged.

If a drug were discovered that could eliminate the need for arduous physical therapy following stroke or spinal injury, it would be hailed by patients and physicians alike, even though patients would lose the character-building opportunity of agonizing rehabilitation exercises. But when someone suggests giving Prozac without psychotherapy to an adult who suffered severe trauma as a child, many therapists wail that this "easy way out" will merely postpone the necessary painful reckoning with the past. Giving shy people medication to ease socializing is dismissed either as pathologizing normal human variation and creating greater conformity or as helping the socially awkward avoid the hard work needed to overcome their fears.

Studies repeatedly find that on their own, drugs and certain talk therapies are about equally effective.

But why should someone who suffered trauma have to suffer more to overcome it, if there's a less difficult, equally safe, and effective alternative? Why shouldn't the shy be on a level playing field with the naturally outgoing if that is what they want? Why is it easier for us to let go of the idea that physical suffering is a message from God that we should bear in order to temper our souls than it is to shake the idea that emotional pain must be endured for our own good?

Considering these questions has helped clarify my thinking about how to deal with my own psychological problems and how to think about the wide variety of psychoactive substances available in our society. As a journalist who covers neuroscience and who has personally experienced some of the brain's aberrant states, I confront these issues almost every day. My chief conclusion is that while psychotherapy validated by research has its place, there is no convincing reason why it should be considered inherently superior to drugs. . . .

Dual Agendas

Although the drug companies clearly have an agenda in pushing their view of psychiatric medication, psychotherapists do too. If pills really could overcome depression and addiction without endless digging and talking they'd be out of business. Just as the "brain chemical imbalance" that supposedly causes depression is part of the pharmaceutical companies' sales pitch, as exemplified by those Zoloft commercials in which a blob with a face turns his frown upside down, the idea that talk is better and deeper and more humanistic is part of the therapists' sales pitch (no matter how much they sincerely believe it).

Suicide rates in the U.S. have declined since the introduction of these drugs.

Each perspective, taken in isolation, relies on an outdated, dualistic view of the mind and brain. The drug companies portray depression as a biological defect that leaves people vulnerable to getting stuck in sadness; the therapists say our thinking and emotional histories trap us there. But neither view precludes the other; both can be right simultaneously because all experience must ultimately be coded by processes in the brain. Given this reality, if the easier, faster way is just as effective, why not use it?

Studies repeatedly find that on their own, drugs and certain talk therapies are about equally effective, with a combination of the two often superior. But the talk therapies which have been proven to work are hard to find. As Vanderbilt University psychologist Steven Hollon puts it, "The treatments shown in clinical trials to be specifically effective for depression are still not widely available."

Side Effects of Medication

Antidepressant opponents such as Peter Breggin argue that drugs can have terrible side effects, so even unproven talk therapies are preferable. Recently, for example, evidence about the relationship between suicide and selective serotonin reuptake inhibitors (SSRIs) such as Prozac and Zoloft has begun to emerge. Not only can they increase suicidal behavior among depressed people, but a study published in 2000 in *Primary*

Care Psychiatry found that some normal people given these medications become suicidal. In clinical trials, suicide rates are two and a half times higher in subjects given SSRIs than in those given placebos, according to David Healy, a psychiatrist at Cardiff University. He estimates that up to 5 percent of the population may have severe negative reactions to SSRIs that can, in the worst cases, lead to suicide.

But that doesn't mean the drugs don't help others. For the majority of patients, SSRIs seem to reduce suicidal thoughts and suicide itself. Suicide rates in the U.S. have declined since the introduction of these drugs. Given that at least 50 million Americans have taken SSRIs since Prozac was approved in 1987, if their main effect was to increase suicide, the opposite should be true. Further, several studies that have compared local SSRI prescribing rates with corresponding suicide rates have found that the medications are linked with fewer, not more, self-inflicted deaths.

Other SSRI critics—such as Harvard psychiatrist Joseph Glenmullen, author of the 2001 book *Prozac Backlash* —note that SSRIs don't seem to have much advantage over placebos in clinical trials. This argument, like the suicide warnings, overlooks the importance of individual variations. . . . When you match the right person to the right medication, the positive change is remarkable and unmistakable. David Healy's research has shown that certain personality traits are associated with extremely positive (and others with extremely negative) reactions to these drugs.

The fact that good matches occur only in a small subset for each drug—and that bad matches occur as well—means that clinical trials wash out the contrast between the drug and placebo groups. Most people have a small positive effect, some are transformed, and some are made worse; grouping them together obscures these differences. Which is why Healy, the author of the 2004 book *Let Them Eat Prozac: The Unhealthy*

Relationship Between the Pharmaceutical Industry and Depression, still prescribes SSRIs and does not want them banned.

Side Effects of Talk Therapy

When it comes to side effects, it's also important to recognize that drugs are not the only treatments that can cause harm. Some forms of psychotherapy can be at least as damaging. . . .

According to research by Yale psychologist Susan Nolen-Hoeksema, depression can be exacerbated by focusing obsessively on "the causes and consequences" of personal problems. Therapies that encourage people to ruminate on the origins of their depression thus can make the condition worse. According to a 1999 study published in the *Journal of Personality and Social Psychology*, many commonly used anger management treatments, which urge clients to "get it out" by yelling and hitting inanimate objects, actually increase rage.

Then there is the matter of all the time and money spent on therapy that could be used for more productive pursuits. [University of California sociologist Richard] Ofshe, who distinguishes between life problems that can be helped by counseling and support and major mental illnesses such as schizophrenia and clinical depression, tells me "all the evidence for years and years has shown that people who practice using psychodynamic techniques, all the therapies derived from Freud, every time anyone tried to treat any real mental disorder, it was a waste of time and money and when real treatment [was developed], they were diverted from something that could be helpful."

Many see such side effects as less problematic than those resulting from drugs, because the patient has a choice whether to follow the therapist's guidance, whereas drug side effects are involuntary. Yet talk therapies cannot work as their proponents intend if the patient doesn't comply, and noncompliance in addiction treatment can result in incarceration, so in that sense the side effects derive just as directly from the treatment.

As Healy points out, talk therapy can "wreck families, can wreck lives just as much as pills can. People tend to see the risks from pills. They think if they [do] talk therapy, there can't be any risk. But no one ever got raped by a Prozac pill."

Although there is no way of knowing how many rapes are committed by mental health professionals, a survey of 1,320 psychologists by researcher Kenneth Pope, published in the journal *Psychotherapy* in 1991, found that at least half of therapists reported treating one or more patients who'd had a sexual relationship with a prior therapist. The respondents believed more than 90 percent of the patients had been harmed by the relationships. Earlier surveys found that between 7 percent and 12 percent of male therapists (including psychiatrists, social workers, and psychologists) admitted to engaging in a sexual relationship with a client at least once.

Antidepressants . . . strengthen the voice that says it's going to be OK.

Strengthening the Voice

Even if drugs outperformed both placebos and talk and had no side effects, there would still remain the complaint that these medications kill pain rather than address its cause. In a 2001 letter to the *Archives of General Psychiatry*, for instance, a psychiatrist described an alcoholic who kept drinking because Prozac made him feel better, leaving him less determined to get sober. The letter also mentioned a woman who lost her resolve to leave an abusive boyfriend after taking Paxil for several weeks.

But while the data from clinical trials of SSRIs in treating addictions are mixed, the findings are either positive effects in reducing alcohol and other drug use or no effect, not reduced recovery. And while some people may remain in abusive relationships because antidepressants dull their desire to get out, others find the courage to leave after being treated with SSRIs. Without better research focused on this issue, it's impossible to know which reaction is more common.

My own experience suggests that whether a drug paralyzes or activates you has as much to do with where you start emotionally as with the drug itself. Some heroin addicts find that the drug (or a maintenance substitute such as methadone) allows them to be kinder and more open to others because it reduces their overwhelming feeling of vulnerability and over-sensitivity; others find it makes them stone cold and numb. It depends on where they begin: If they are too self-conscious and anxious to socialize, lowering the volume of those sensations can help; if they are already indifferent, the drug will make that worse.

Antidepressants are similar. Although they don't offer the unearned euphoria that so disturbs anti-drug crusaders, they do, like heroin, strengthen the voice that says its going to be OK, which is so important for getting through tough times and which some people may not be able to access without chemical help.

Tough Love?

It's the same with physical pain: Too much agony can be as life-destroying and consciousness contracting as too much anesthesia, and the determination of how much is too much depends both on the original level of pain and on how the drug changes it. Just consider whether you are more agreeable to and nurturant of your loved ones when you have a ferocious toothache, or when the pain has been properly medicated. One cannot discuss a good or a bad drug—only a good or bad drug for a specific person and purpose.

The notion that emotional pain and difficulties inevitably lead to growth and maturity is a largely unexamined assumption with deeps roots in Western religion. Almost everyone can name individuals who believe their painful challenges made them into better people. This is part of why "tough love" approaches to emotional problems continue to thrive and why "easier, softer" approaches such as medication are so often dismissed. As Fox News Channel commentator Sean Hannity put it in 2002, "I've had a criticism of [psychiatrists] for a long time. I think they're too quick to overprescribe drugs and offer chemical solutions. They totally discount the spiritual side of the human nature."

But such critics rarely consider how often pain truly leads to growth—and how often it leads to stagnation, self-destructive escape attempts, and greater emotional damage. Few question whether the anecdote of the survivor made stronger is more common than that of the victim devastated. Most people can easily cite examples of both. Since pain is so common, however, we want to think it's essential to growth. We want it to *mean something* —and don't like to imagine we could learn to be happier, better people without it. . . .

Dependence Worries

One final argument for preferring talk to drugs is fear of dependence. Some antidepressant drugs do produce painful withdrawal symptoms, and it is unconscionable that some patients are given these medications without appropriate warnings and without first having tried other, less problematic treatments. But there's also no doubt that some talk therapies create dependence every bit as worrisome. Just think of those analysands [psychiatric patients] who have therapy four hours a week and never make a decision without first consulting their shrinks.

While it's always better to have fewer needs, physical dependence on medication, in and of itself, needn't be a problem if the drug is readily available and safe. If the drug improves one's ability to work and love, who is being hurt?

We're all dependent on air, food, and water, and maintenance medications will become a fact of life for most of us as we outlive the ages which our bodies evolved to reach. Whether the medication treats high blood pressure, pain, or depression shouldn't matter.

Medication Is Not the Only Answer

This is not to say we have anything close to perfect medications—and for many people, the tradeoff between side effects, risks, and benefits weighs against taking those currently available. In this connection, full disclosure of the data on current drugs and more research and openness on those in development is critical.

Nor do I believe there is never lingering emotional distress that needs to be understood and conquered, or that there is no role for talk therapy or self-help. Many studies, including a 2002 review in the *American Journal of Psychiatry* and a more recent head-to-head trial published [in 2005] in the same journal, have found that certain talk therapies are just as effective as drugs. A 2003 study published in the *Proceedings of the National Academy of Sciences* even found that for people with childhood trauma, one such therapy was more effective.

Mental health professionals need to understand that suffering isn't necessarily good for the soul.

But evidence-based therapy is hard to find outside university research studies. The therapy that helped the childhood trauma victims more than drugs, for example, was a cognitive-behavioral treatment that focused on dealing with current problems, not searching for their roots in the past. It wasn't the kind of "depth" treatment talk therapy proponents usually advocate.

Few patients outside of studies get therapy based on what the research finds effective; most practitioners ignore the data and do what their "clinical experience" suggests. Recognizing this gap, government agents such as the Substance Abuse and Mental Health Services Administration have distributed literature and sponsored initiatives aimed at bringing "research into practice." But while the situation is far better than it was 10 or even five years ago, both researchers and patients say there's a long way to go. For talk therapy to be a genuine alternative or supplement to medication, the methods covered by insurers should be proven safe and effective, just as the Food and Drug Administration requires for drugs. Mental health advocates have long called for "parity" between coverage of mental and physical illnesses, but it makes no sense to cover talk unless therapists practice proven treatments.

Equal Value, Equal Pitfalls

In addition to insisting on evidence of effectiveness, mental health professionals need to understand that suffering isn't necessarily good for the soul. My own experience has shown me that therapy, self-help, and medication all have value. It has also shown me the pitfalls of each. Both depression and addiction have biological, sociological, and psychological dimensions that vary in importance depending upon the individual and his or her situation. This complexity means that no one solution will work in all cases and that the right approach for any given person may change over time.

I can say this: Painful talk therapy isn't morally superior to medication or to therapy that doesn't go "deep." Pleasure can be just as important for emotional recovery and growth as pain, if not more so. That's why drugs sometimes are the better fix.

5

Children Are Overmedicated with ADHD Drugs

Bruce Wiseman

Bruce Wiseman is president of the U.S. branch of the Citizens Commission on Human Rights International (CCHR), an organization established by the Church of Scientology to investigate and expose human rights violations by the psychiatric profession.

While there are undoubtedly children who suffer from learning and behavioral difficulties and need psychiatric drugs, far too many young people are being incorrectly diagnosed and unnecessarily medicated. Millions of children are being prescribed stimulants and antidepressants for ADHD (attention deficit hyperactivity disorder), in spite of abundant medical evidence that such drugs have dangerous short-term and long-term effects. One of the reasons these drugs are overprescribed is the inherent ambiguity in an ADHD diagnosis. As medical professionals have long acknowledged, there are no objective criteria for determining whether a child has ADHD. Furthermore, the symptoms of ADHD have many possible causes, from sleep apnea to lead poisoning. Ultimately, parents of children who truly have learning or behavioral problems have a right to be informed of all treatment options and choose the option that best suits their child.

Bruce Wiseman, "Hearing on Attention Deficit/Hyperactivity Disorder—Are We Overmedicating Our Children?" testimony before the House Committee on Government Reform, September 26, 2002.

No one can disagree that the health and welfare of children and their families are priorities for any country.

For over 30 years, CCHR's observations and conclusions have been drawn from speaking to hundreds of thousands of parents, doctors, teachers and others who have reported human rights abuse in the mental health system, especially against children.

For example, at seven, Matthew Smith was diagnosed through his school as having Attention Deficit Hyperactivity Disorder (ADHD). His parents were told that he needed to take a stimulant to help him focus. Initially resistant, Matthew's parents were told that non-compliance could bring criminal charges for neglecting their son's educational and emotional needs. "My wife and I were scared of the possibility of losing our children if we didn't comply," said Matthew's father, Lawrence Smith. They conceded to the pressure.

On March 21, 2000, while skateboarding, Matthew tragically died from a heart attack. The coroner determined that he had died from the long-term use of the *prescribed* stimulant.

We all know that there *are* children who are troubled, who do need care. But what that "care" is or should be is the point of contention.

In 1999—in the wake of the Columbine school shootings—CCHR worked with Colorado State Board of Education member, Mrs. Patty Johnson, who orchestrated the passage of the precedent-setting school board resolution that recommended academic rather than drug solutions for behavioral and learning problems in the classroom. Teenage shooters Eric Harris and Dylan Klebold had undergone psychological "anger management classes" and Harris was taking an antidepressant known to cause mania.

Mrs. Johnson stated, "The diagnosing of children with ... mental disorders is not the role of school personnel, nor is recommending the use of psychiatric drugs. ... The

[Colorado] resolution told educators that their role was to teach and to pursue academic and disciplinary solutions for problems of attention and learning."

The Journal of the American Medical Association reported that methylphenidate (Ritalin) acts much like cocaine.

Then in 2000, Jennifer L. Wood, Chief Legal Counsel for the Rhode Island Department of Education, issued a letter to all school superintendents stating that the federal *Individuals with Disabilities in Education Act* (IDEA) "prohibits school personnel from making a decision about a child's educational services without the consent of the child's parent(s). School personnel must refrain from making statements that may be construed as offering medical advice, or making a medical decision, such as 'Your child should be taking medication,' or 'I've seen many students like your child and based on that experience your child should be on medication'. . . . It is not lawful for school personnel to require that a child continue or initiate a course of taking medication as a condition of attending school. School personnel cannot require, suggest or imply that a student take medication as a condition of attending school."

Yet this is violated across the nation.

Dangerous Drugs

Millions of children are being drugged with powerful stimulants and antidepressants, placing our nation's children at risk. There are scores of studies that substantiate this. In testimony before a 1970 Congressional Hearing on whether or not to fund research into pharmacological treatment for school problems, Dr. John D. Griffith, Assistant Professor of Psychiatry, Vanderbilt University School of Medicine, stated: "I would like to point out that every drug, however innocuous, has some degree of toxicity. A drug, therefore, is a type of poison and its poisonous qualities must be carefully weighed against its therapeutic usefulness. A problem, now being considered in most of the capitols of the Free World, is whether the benefits derived from amphetamines outweigh their toxicity. It is the consensus of the World Scientific Literature that the amphetamines are of very little benefit to mankind. They are, however, quite toxic.

In 2000, *The Journal of the American Academy of Child and Adolescent Psychiatry* reported, "It is well known that psycho-stimulants have abuse potential. Very high doses of psycho-stimulants . . . may cause central nervous system damage, cardiovascular damage, and hypertension. In addition, high doses have been associated with compulsive behaviors, and in certain vulnerable individuals, movement disorders."

In August 2001, the *Journal of the American Medical Association* reported that methylphenidate (Ritalin) acts much like cocaine. Injected as a liquid, it sends a jolt that "addicts like very much," said Nora Volkow, M.D., psychiatrist and imaging expert at Brookhaven National Laboratory, Upton, NY. The drug is chemically similar to cocaine, the study says. It also admits that although psychiatrists have used this drug to treat ADHD for 40 years, they and pharmacologists have never known how or why it worked.

Corrective Legislation

As a result of over-medicating our children and the fact that so many parents were being forced to place their child on such drugs through our schools, currently more than half of our states have introduced and/or passed some type of legislation or regulation to restrict the use of psychiatric drugs for children. [In 2000] the Texas State Board of Education passed a resolution indicating that Ritalin prescribed for ADHD resulted in "little improvement in academic or social skills," and "psychiatric prescription drugs have been utilized for what are essentially problems of discipline which may be related to lack of academic success." Among a number of recommendations, it urged schools to "use proven academic and/or management solutions to resolve behavior, attention, and learning difficulties" and recommended that parents be informed of programs such as "tutoring, vision testing, phonics, nutritional guidance, medical examinations, allergy testing, standard disciplinary procedures, and other remedies known to be effective and harmless." . . .

A Questionable Diagnosis

The Model Legislation adopted by the National Foundation of Women Legislators Education Policy Committee, quotes from a report by the 1998 NIH [National Institutes of Health] Conference on the Diagnosis and Treatment of ADHD. This, in part, concluded, "We don't have an independent, valid test for ADHD; there are no data to indicate that ADHD is due to a brain malfunction . . . and finally, after years of clinical research and experience with ADHD, our knowledge about the cause or causes of ADHD remains speculative."

Even the Surgeon General's 1999 report on mental health said that the exact etiology (cause) for ADHD is unknown. Indeed, the Surgeon General said, "The diagnosis of mental disorders is often believed to be more difficult than diagnosis of somatic or general medical disorders *since there is no definitive lesion, laboratory test or abnormality in brain tissue that can identify illness.*" (emphasis added)

In August [2002], the Netherlands Advertising Code Commission ordered the country's Brain Foundation to cease advertising ADHD as a brain dysfunction, stating, "The information that the defendant presented gives no grounds for the definitive statement that ADHD is an inherent brain dysfunction. . . . Under the circumstances, the defendant has not been careful enough and the advertisement is misleading."

This is, perhaps, the crux of the problem—that we are relying on a diagnosis that is subjective and is open to arbitrary use and abuse. The symptoms of ADHD could be caused by anything from normal childhood antics to toxic or allergic reactions to too much sugar.

Other Possible Causes

Dr. Arthur Teng of the Sydney Children's Hospital says that sleep apnea "can have a very big impact on a child's behavior, learning ability and attention during the day."

According to Dr. Mark Filidel from the Whitaker Wellness Center in California, the symptoms of lead poisoning are "strikingly similar to several psychiatric 'diseases' [and] can exhibit . . . learning disorders, hyperactivity, aggressive or disruptive behavior."

Toxic chemicals contribute to learning or behavioral problems, including lead, mercury, industrial chemicals, and certain pesticides.

Evidence reviewed by the National Academy of Sciences [in 2002] indicates that toxic chemicals contribute to learning or behavioral problems, including lead, mercury, industrial chemicals, and certain pesticides. A University of Arizona study found that children exposed to a combination of pesticides before birth and through breast milk exhibited less stamina, and poorer memory and coordination, than other kids.

There are so many potential causes for a child's learning or behavioral problems that to deny parents all the information about these is neglect in itself. . . .

In May [2002], the Council of Europe, which investigated the misdiagnosing and drugging of children in response to concerns about American child drugging trends emerging in

Europe, issued its findings, which included: "The Assembly also considers that more research should be conducted into the impact of proper tutoring and educational solutions for children exhibiting ADHD symptoms, into the behavioral effects of such medical problems as allergies or toxic reactions, and into alternative forms of treatment such as diet."

Are ADHD Children Merely Gifted?

Furthermore, thousands of children put on psychiatric drugs are simply "smart." The late Dr. Sydney Walker, psychiatrist, neurologist and author said [in his 1998 book, *The Hyperactivity Hoax*], "They're hyper not because their brains don't work right, but because they spend most of the day waiting for slower students to catch up with them. These students are bored to tears, and people who are bored fidget, wiggle, scratch, stretch, and (especially if they are boys) start looking for ways to get into trouble."

Also consider the similarities between the signs of giftedness and "learning" and "behavioral disorders."

Giftedness:

- Poor attention, boredom, daydreaming in specific situations
- Low tolerance for persistence on tasks that seem irrelevant
- Judgment lags behind development of intellect
- Intensity may lead to power struggles with authorities
- High activity level; may need less sleep
- Questions rules, customs and traditions

Compare to Behavior Associated with ADHD

- Poorly sustained attention in almost all situations
- Diminished persistence on tasks without immediate consequences
- Impulsivity, poor delay of gratification

- Impaired adherence to commands to regulate or inhibit behavior in social contexts
- More active, restless than other children
- Difficulty adhering to rules and regulations

What Is a Disability?

No legislation should allow for the drugging of children, especially the enforced drugging of children, to be based on the arbitrariness of today's "Learning Disorders" diagnostic criteria.

For example, the President's Commission on Excellence in Education revealed [in 2002] that 40 percent of kids are being labeled with "learning disorders" simply because they have not been taught to read. State and federal governments spend $28 billion per year for educating children categorized under the label, "Non Specific Learning Disorder."

According to pediatric neurologist, Dr. Fred Baughman, Jr., "The most fundamental aspect of reforming the IDEA is to provide a definitive physically based definition of disability. This must include the necessity to establish a tangible, objective physical abnormality which can be determined by a test such as, but not limited to, blood or urine test, x-ray, brain scan or biopsy. If none of these learning 'disorders' can meet this test, then clearly there is no physical abnormality and we are labeling entirely normal children as abnormal."

Millions of children are being told there is something "wrong" with their brain, although no one can prove it.

Ensuring Informed Consent

All this information should be made available to parents when making an informed choice about the medical or educational needs of their child. This is in keeping with U.S. Public Law 96-88, which states, "Parents have the primary responsibility for the education of their children, and States, localities, and private institutions have the primary responsibility for supporting that parental role."

And it would align with the American Medical Association's standard for informed consent, which calls for communicating the "nature and purpose of a proposed treatment or procedure; the risks and benefits" of such treatments and the *alternatives*. . . ." In relation to parental permission and assent in pediatric practice, The American Academy of Pediatrics also notes that ". . .the patient has the freedom to choose among the medical alternatives without coercion or manipulation."

Millions of children are being told there is something 'wrong' with their brain, although no one can prove it. They are labeled "mentally disordered" with diagnoses that are subjective and then subjected to potentially dangerous and addicting drugs in order to control or change their behavior, a stigmatizing process to say the least. . . .

Families are grieving for their lost children because they were not provided with all the facts about mental health treatments, especially psychotropic drugs, and were denied access to alternative and workable solutions.

6

Children with ADHD Are Not Overmedicated

E. Clarke Ross

E. Clarke Ross is chief executive officer of Children and Adults with Attention-Deficit/Hyperactivity Disorder (CHADD), the nation's leading advocacy group for individuals with attention deficit/hyperactivity disorder and their families.

When the author's son, Andrew, was diagnosed with attention deficit/hyperactivity disorder (ADHD), numerous treatment options were explored before Andrew's parents agreed to a psychiatrist's recommendation that Andrew try a stimulant medication. The third medication tried showed significant results, and Andrew, now eleven, still takes it. Claims that children like Andrew can be adequately treated with structure, discipline, and counseling and that they should not be helped with medication are insulting. Many critics even go so far as to say that ADHD is not a legitimate disorder—a claim that is clearly contradicted by scientific evidence. While there have been instances of children being haphazardly diagnosed and prescribed stimulant medications, the evidence shows that underdiagnosis of ADHD is actually a more prevalent problem than overdiagnosis. As a result, a multitude of children suffering from ADHD are not getting the treatment—including medications—that could dramatically improve their lives.

E. Clarke Ross, "Hearing on Attention Deficit/Hyperactivity Disorders—Are We Overmedicating Our Children?", testimony before the House Committee on Government Reform, September 26, 2002.

[I am] father to an eleven-year-old son, Andrew, diagnosed with the inattentive type of AD/HD, an anxiety disorder, and other related co-occurring learning disorders.

Like many families facing AD/HD and related conditions, my wife and I, over time, have employed a wide array of interventions, including several considered complementary in nature, which are described in greater detail further in this statement. None of the complementary interventions we employed were harmful. But perhaps most significant, none of them have demonstrated an impact. Moreover, none of them are supported by the evidence-based research to which we are firmly committed.

In short, the multi-modal approach /... parent training in diagnosis, treatment and specific behavior management techniques, an appropriate educational program, individual and family counseling when needed and, for us, medication provided and continue to provide the support that Andrew needs in order to thrive and flourish.

Andrew was born following a complicated delivery. When at age 11 months, he broke his ankle (which would not heal properly), follow-up assessments documented significant hypotonia and sensory integration challenges. At 21 months, he experienced his first unprovoked seizure with a pattern of seizures continuing for the next several years. Two EEGs [electroencephalograms, tests used to detect abnormal electrical activity in the brain] later, many problems were confirmed. By two and still not speaking, Andrew's pediatrician referred him to the State of Maryland's Early Education Program. For the next several years he received intensive speech and language and sensory integration services. Andrew also has dysgraphia, which can best be described as a difficulty in automatically remembering and mastering the sequence of muscle motor movements needed in writing letters or numbers. Fortunately, with intensive assistance from the school occupational therapist, Andrew has largely overcome his dysgraphia.

Impeded Abilities

By four, when Andrew entered a more formal education program, teachers began noting significant learning problems stemming directly from his inability to focus. He received numerous independent professional assessments, each affirming that his disabilities significantly impeded his ability to function at the level of his classmates. Andrew has always had difficulty with what now is referred to as "executive functioning"—brain actions of self control where he is unable to think ahead and consider "if-then" behaviors and their consequences.

My son does not have an occasional problem with distraction and attention. He has ongoing, continuous daily problems that result in overwhelming difficulties in many areas of his life.

By the time Andrew was seven, we said yes to stimulant medication. The other interventions had not worked.

No well-meaning parent sets out to medicate his or her child. Nor did we. But over time, given Andrew's learning and functional problems, we accepted the advice of child psychiatrists who felt our son would benefit from medication. Today, Andrew takes both a medication for attention issues and a medication designed to reduce his anxiety. A series of behavioral management and learning assistance programs also are used and are an essential part of his overall treatment program.

At age four, a child psychiatrist recommended that Andrew try a stimulant medication. We initially said no, as we wanted to first try other interventions. But by the time Andrew was seven, we said yes to stimulant medication. The other interventions had not worked in helping him pay attention. We now were ready to try medication.

We actually tried three medications before we found one that worked. The first two did not help his attention (nor did they have any side effects), but the third one did have significant results. To this day Andrew takes Adderall.

Multimodal Treatment

Andrew began using Prozac two and a half years ago because of a severe anxiety problem. He is anxious about many things. As one example of many, Andrew was so afraid of flying insects that three summers ago he would not go outside despite his love of baseball and basketball. A combination of behavioral interventions, cognitive training and medication has helped to reduce his anxiety. He remains uncomfortable with flying insects and bristles stiffly when they are around, but generally speaking he now can function quite normally. But his anxiety was not singularly confined to flying insects. Andrew is anxious about many things and many situations. As such, my wife and I are constantly developing behavioral interventions to deal with these varied anxieties.

Medication obviously is not perfect. For example, Andrew initially experienced a significant loss in appetite. Today, however, he only experiences a loss of appetite at lunch, proof that there are continual tradeoffs in the beneficial use of medication and side effects from such use. On the plus side, however, with the assistance of special education personnel and a multimodal treatment approach in place, including medication, Andrew can now better attend to learning in class, is less phobic, and demonstrates more socially appropriate behaviors with children his age.

As the parent of a child with multiple challenges, I resent those who suggest that my son needs only a little more discipline, structure, and learning. I want to emphatically say that my son's problems are neither "lies" nor "frauds" nor the "failures of his parents." Andrew has a biologically based brain disorder that we and an extensive network of dedicated clinicians face and address on a daily basis. Andrew's life is filled with dedicated clinicians—from pediatrician, to child psychiatrist, to child psychologist, to neurologist, to speech pathologist, to a team of educators. Without their collective support, I cannot imagine where Andrew would be today.

Making Progress

As mentioned previously, we employ a variety of complementary approaches. These include visualizing and verbalizing training, sensory integration therapy, and visual tracking. Andrew responds best in small learning groups where constant feedback and support is provided. We use Dr. Thomas Phelan's 1-2-3 Magic approaches each and every day. And every day Andrew consumes fish oil supplements (Omega-3 Fatty Acids). But as noted above, while certainly not harmful, none of these interventions (other than 1-2-3 Magic) have yielded any immediate or even long-lasting positive impact upon Andrew.

The good news is that Andrew is making progress. The strides are slow yet steady. And like most families in similar circumstances, we are resolved to living life one day at a time. I share my wife's and my story with the hope that those unfamiliar with AD/HD will appreciate the complexity and difficulty of identifying and implementing key medical strategies designed to help children like our son Andrew.

In 1999, the U.S. Surgeon General released ... [a report that stated] that stimulants are highly effective for 75–90% of children with AD/HD.

Evidence-Based Science

In looking at the broader AD/HD picture—particularly with respect to the emergence of evidence-based science—it is essential to note the following key milestones:

- In 1998, the American Medical Association published an exhaustive review of the scientific literature concerning AD/HD, concluding that the disorder is real and that while there may be instances of overdiagnosis, *there is a greater problem of underdiagnosis.*

• In 1999, the National Institute of Mental Health (NIMH) published its first results from The Multimodal Treatment Study of Children with Attention-Deficit/ Hyperactivity Disorder, a multicenter study evaluating the leading treatments for ADHD, including various forms of behavior therapy and medications, in nearly 600 elementary school children. The results indicate that long-term combination treatments as well as medication management alone are both significantly superior to intensive behavioral treatments and routine community treatments in reducing AD/HD symptoms.

• In 1999, the U.S. Surgeon General released the landmark Report on Mental Health, which devotes an entire section to the evidence-based science behind AD/HD. Among the important findings are that stimulants are highly effective for 75–90% of children with AD/HD, while the most effective interventions for AD/HD are multimodal treatment—which involves the use of medication with psychosocial, behavioral and related interventions. Finally, "recent reports found little evidence of overdiagnosis of AD/HD or overprescription of stimulant medications. Indeed fewer children (2–3% of school-aged children) are being treated for AD/HD than suffer from it."

• First in 2000 for assessment, and then in 2001 for treatment, the American Academy of Pediatrics (AAP) published clinical practice guidelines for AD/HD. These groundbreaking guidelines include endorsement of stimulant medications when appropriate monitoring and behavior interventions are also used.

• In 2002, the American Academy of Child and Adolescent Psychiatry (AACAP) published practice parameters for the use of stimulant medications in the treatment of children, adolescents and adults. The parameters rely on an evidence-based medicine approach derived from a detailed literature review and expert opinion.

The Prevalence of AD/HD

In reviewing the developments above, it is simultaneously essential to note that both U.S. Surgeon General's reports on mental health (1999 on mental health research, and the 2001 report on race and culture) emphasize that some children are inappropriately identified while many children are *never* identified.

It therefore also becomes essential to comment upon public alarm that "AD/HD is over-identified and over-medicated" because of the over 700% increase in the use of stimulant medication in the school age population over the past decade. Before resorting to alarmist reactions, let us first examine the prevalence rate.

- The U.S. Surgeon General estimates the school-age prevalence of AD/HD to be between 3 and 5%. Even with the over 700% increase in stimulant medication use over the past decade, only 2 to 2.5% of the school-age population currently receive stimulant medication. If medication is an appropriate component of multimodal intervention (as the science informs us), then over half of those suffering the effects of AD/HD are not being effectively treated.

- The 3-to-5% prevalence rate may actually be a conservative rate. Two published studies by the Mayo Clinic of Rochester, Minnesota, one in the January 2001 issue of the *Journal of the American Medical Association* and the other in the March 2002 issue of the *Archives of Pediatrics and Adolescent Medicine* documented that 7.5% of all children presenting for any kind of medical treatment in Rochester over a seven year period had AD/HD.

What is particularly alarming to CHADD [Children and Adults with Attention-Deficit/Hyperactivity Disorder] is the tremendous variance of stimulant medication prescribing practices across the nation. While Dr. Julie Zito of the University of Maryland and Dr. Gretchen LeFever of Eastern Virginia Medical School have published studies about the significant variance within Maryland and Virginia, probably the single most informative published study was the May 6, 2001 *Cleveland Plain Dealer* article, "Ritalin Prescribed Unevenly in U.S." The paper's reporters studied for one full year the actual prescriptions written in every county in the nation. Some counties had 5% of the total school-age population and 20% of school-age boys on stimulant medication while other counties had practically no one receiving a stimulant medication. CHADD remains alarmed with this variance of practice.

Alarmist statements and reports create confusion among the general public . . . thus undermining the seriousness of AD/HD and the proven safety and efficacy of stimulant medications.

Why the Variance in Treatment?

CHADD believes that the single most important reason for such variance is the absence in clinical practice of the use of the AAP and AACAP evidence-based assessment and treatment guidelines. That is why CHADD is tirelessly working to educate the public about the AAP and AACAP guidelines and to advocate that physicians using such guidelines be financially reimbursed by health insurance payers at a higher rate than physicians not using such guidelines.

We also need better research about the prevalence of AD/HD and the number of children actually receiving such medication. While the *Cleveland Plain Dealer* and others have studied the numbers of prescriptions written, we really have no excellent database on actual numbers of children receiving such medications on a regular basis. Certainly, we must protect the confidentiality of individual children and their families, but we also need better aggregate data on overall usage.

For example, consider the data. The United States General Accounting Office in 2001 stated that there were 46.6 million public school students. Three-to-five percent of this total would be between 1.4 to 2.3 million children, not including students in both private school or home-school settings. If we use the Mayo Clinic 7.5% prevalence rate, then 3.26 million school age children would be expected to have AD/HD—an appropriate number given such rates. CHADD commends the Centers for Disease Control and Prevention (CDC) for recognizing the need to better assess accurate prevalence rates, including funding for three prevalence studies.

The Key Role of Physicians, Teachers, and Families

CHADD is concerned that without proper context, and when sensationalized, alarmist statements and reports create confusion among the general public, patients and families, thus undermining the seriousness of AD/HD and the proven safety and efficacy of stimulant medications when properly administered by appropriate professionals.

CHADD believes that all families should have access to the best, evidence-based science in the diagnosis and treatment of AD/HD. We are therefore concerned when legislation is proposed that undermines this critical access—including the elimination of a teacher's freedom to recommend a comprehensive and complete medical assessment by persons licensed to perform such evaluations. Likewise, CHADD is appalled when children are inappropriately prescribed medication that they do not need. This is of particular concern when small subsets of children suffer significant side effects.

CHADD believes that legislation must not limit or undermine the ability of a medical professional, within their scope of practice, from treating AD/HD based on the most widely accepted evidence-based science. CHADD encourages all families and physicians to follow best practice assessment and treatment guidelines being uniformly implemented throughout the nation, specifically the current American Academy of Pediatrics (AAP) and American Academy of Child and Adolescent Psychiatry (AACAP) guidelines. Using the force of law and agencies of government—particularly criminal penalties—to monitor and enforce best practice treatment guidelines is an ineffective approach at best and a disastrous approach at worst. Instead, ongoing training and education in the diagnosis and treatment of AD/HD should be encouraged among all physicians.

Teachers are frequently the first to recognize learning, functioning, and behavioral problems in the school setting and therefore should be able to advise parents of such observations. CHADD believes that professionals should act within their professional scope of practice. Thus, school personnel should not recommend the use of medication. Medication assessment and prescription is the role of the physician and— under limited circumstances—in a few states, other treating professionals too. However, teachers should be able to recommend a comprehensive and complete medical assessment by persons licensed to perform such evaluations.

Because students spend a significant portion of their day in the classroom, the vital role that teachers play in providing observations to the diagnosing professionals cannot be underestimated. Effective communication among teachers, professionals and parents is essential and strongly encouraged. CHADD advocates a multimodal approach to the treatment of AD/HD, including parent training in diagnosis, treatment and specific behavior management techniques, an appropriate educational program, individual and family counseling when needed, and medication when required. Medication is used to improve the symptoms of AD/HD. Research shows that children and adults who take medication for the symptoms of AD/HD attribute their successes to themselves, not to the medication.

Denial of AD/HD

The organized interests . . . claiming that AD/HD is a "biological lie" also state that there are no "biological imbalances" and "no laboratory tests established as diagnostic" for AD/HD. They go on to claim that AD/HD is a "100 percent fraud."

Instead of wasting precious time, energy and resources defending a disorder that clearly exists, why can't we simply move forward?

But science tells us a different story. The Surgeon General's report ["Mental Health: A Report of the Surgeon General," 1999] . . . concludes, "AD/HD is the most commonly diagnosed behavioral disorder in childhood and occurs in three to five percent of all school-age children. The exact etiology of AD/HD is unknown, although neurotransmitter deficits (such as the dopamine transmitter), genetics, and perinatal complications have been implicated." The NIH [National Institutes of Health] Panel Consensus statement declares: "Although an independent diagnostic test for AD/HD does not exist, there is evidence supporting the validity of the disorder."

As previously stated, the NIMH MTA Study further documented that only 31% of the children with AD/HD have AD/HD alone with no other disorder. The study found that 40% of children with AD/HD had oppositional defiant disorder, 34% had anxiety disorder, 14% had conduct disorder, and 4% had a mood disorder. Those dismissing the existence of AD/HD repeatedly ignore these characteristics. A May 22

[2002] study by the Centers for Disease Control and Prevention (CDC) documented that half of the school age population with AD/HD also had a learning disability.

The existence of co-occurring disorders complicates assessment, complicates treatment, and increases the possibility of an inaccurate diagnosis. This only further reiterates the importance of the AAP and AACAP best practice guidelines.

Facing the Reality of AD/HD

I have devoted over 30 years of my professional life assisting individuals with cerebral palsy, schizophrenia, bipolar disorder, AD/HD, and other mental disorders. I find it frustrating and disheartening that I have to defend recognized science against science fiction. This is demeaning to those suffering from these disorders and to the millions of families who devote their lives caring for and supporting their loved ones.

The science speaks for itself. Even more important are the stories of untold millions who have either been helped by appropriate interventions—or worse, been denied access to the treatment they deserve. Instead of wasting precious time, energy and resources defending a disorder that clearly exists, why can't we simply move forward in applying the science to clinical practice and educational settings to make life better for those faced with these challenges? Why do some policy makers continue to play to those who claim that there are no mental disorders, that there is no science, and that anyone's science fiction is equivalent to the evidence-based science?

The reality that children and adolescents can and do suffer from AD/HD and other debilitating brain disorders, just as adults do, is finally being widely recognized. That is why we must continue educating others and ourselves about the broad spectrum of childhood mental disorders. We must continue joining forces with the scientific institutions and others. And we must do everything within our means to ensure that our children receive the tools they need to live a meaningful life, regardless of their disability, challenge or disorder.

7

Prescription Drug Advertising Leads to Overmedication

Peter Lurie

Peter Lurie is a physician and deputy director of Public Citizen's Health Research Group, an advocacy group founded by consumer advocate Ralph Nader.

Since the Food and Drug Administration (FDA) relaxed restrictions on pharmaceutical companies' advertisements aimed directly at consumers (rather than physicians) in 1997, Americans have been inundated with print and broadcast advertisements for prescription drugs. However, harm caused by direct-to-consumer advertising strongly outweighs its alleged benefits. Predictions that direct-to-consumer advertising would lead to patients demanding specific medications from their doctors have proven to be true. As a result of these ads, doctors are prescribing unnecessary medications. At the same time, direct-to-consumer advertising has not led to patients with undertreated conditions being better diagnosed. In order to protect consumers, the FDA should approve patient information for all prescription drugs. Along with other government agencies, the FDA should also do more to educate patients about prescription drugs instead

Peter Lurie, "Hearing on the Impact of Direct-to-Consumer Drug Advertising on Seniors' Health and Health Care Costs," testimony before the Senate Special Committee on Aging, September 29, 2005.

of allowing the pharmaceutical companies to have a monopoly on providing prescription medication information.

L ike all interventions in health care, direct-to-consumer (DTC) advertising should be evaluated by comparing its risks to its benefits, in the context of the available or potentially available alternatives. The objective, of course, is to realize the potential benefits while minimizing the risks. On balance, we believe that the clearly demonstrated adverse effects of DTC advertising outweigh the still-undemonstrated, theoretical benefits of the advertising. Every country in the world has reached this conclusion, except the United States. Only New Zealand has ever permitted DTC advertising, but it imposed a moratorium in December 2004. The European Union considered permitting DTC advertising, but rejected the idea.

Bribing physicians to prescribe medications has long been held to be illegal.

Predictably, DTC advertising has been concentrated on new, expensive drugs for conditions that are bothersome and incurable. Thus, according to the Government Accounting Office (GAO), the top 15 DTC-advertised drugs in 2000 accounted for 54% of all DTC advertising expenditures. Only 14% of sales for the top 50 DTC-advertised drugs is for acute conditions and only one of the top 50 DTC-advertised drugs was an antibiotic, presumably because patients are generally cured and have no need for refills. Most are targeted at seniors. Strikingly, one never encounters advertisements for generic drugs, even though, for example, generic diuretics are the most cost-effective method for preventing heart attacks and stroke. Because patient entreaties are unlikely to induce a physician to initiate or change a prescription for a cancer drug, these are also less likely to be advertised. Of course, DTC advertising shoulders aside non-drug interventions such as behavioral smoking cessation, weight-loss or exercise programs, which can be less costly, safer or more effective. In sum, there is little relationship between our true public health needs and the subjects of DTC advertising.

Many DTC Ads Are Misleading or Dangerous

In the eight years since the FDA opened the floodgates to broadcast DTC advertising, numerous inappropriate advertisements have appeared. The most widely discussed have been the massive DTC campaigns waged by the manufacturers of the Cox-2 inhibitors. Importantly, these drugs were never proved to be more effective pain relievers than many drugs available over-the-counter. For most patients the purported stomach protection offered by these drugs (a claim that the FDA permitted only for Vioxx, but through industry promotional efforts came to be associated with the other Cox-2 inhibitors as well) was irrelevant as those patients tolerated conventional pain relievers without stomach upset. Nonetheless, an estimated two-thirds of the growth in Cox-2 use between 1999 and 2000 was among such patients. In 2000, Vioxx was the number one DTC-advertised drug—at $160 million, larger than the campaigns that year for Pepsi and Budweiser—and retail sales quadrupled. With as many as 140,000 serious cardiovascular events due to Vioxx alone, the dangers of such promotions are now increasingly apparent. Other drugs that have been transformed from pedestrian to blockbuster in part by DTC advertising are Claritin for allergies and Singulair for asthma.

One of the more astounding DTC advertisements we have seen is . . . still running. Produced by Galderma Laboratories, the makers of the prescription acne medication Differin (adapalene), and broadcast both on the Internet and on MTV, the advertisements direct teenage viewers to a portion of the Differin website to receive free music downloads. The advertisements are clearly directed at teenagers: the viewer is exhorted to obtain a Teen Survival Handbook and to take a self-test on acne called Zit 101, a course on offer at Acne High. The advertisement plays to teenage fears ("Remember: There are thousands of pores on your face, which means your skin has the potential to 'give birth to' thousands of microcomedones.") and notions of empowerment ("Fight Acne with Free Music. How Cool Is That?"). Realizing that many teens will visit physicians only with their parents, the website has an entire section on "Talking to Parents About Acne." If you can convince your parent to help you secure a prescription for Differin, the benefits multiply: the "3 levels of cool" are Level 1: sign up (two free music downloads); Level 2: get and fill Differin prescription (seven free downloads); and Level 3: refill Differin prescription (ten free downloads). Bribing physicians to prescribe medications has long been held to be illegal. This advertisement essentially pays teenagers to convince adults to procure this drug for them, with the size of the payment in proportion to the amount of drug prescribed. Incidentally, a previous Differin DTC advertisement has already been the subject of an FDA regulatory letter.

An improbable new low in inappropriate DTC advertising was reached in a November 2004 advertisement by AstraZeneca on its website and in print that actually had the audacity to mislead the public by misrepresenting the FDA. In an advertisement for the cholesterol-lowering drug Crestor, a drug associated with muscle and kidney damage, AstraZeneca claimed that "We have been assured today at senior levels in the FDA that there is no concern in relation to CRESTOR's safety." [Lobbying organization] Public Citizen wrote to the FDA pointing out that the agency was actually on record stating that "[the Agency] has been very concerned about Crestor since the day it was approved, and we've been watching it very carefully." The agency forced the company to terminate its campaign.

Consumers Misled, Doctors Coerced

Consumers have many misconceptions about DTC advertising. In one survey, 50% believed that DTC advertisements had to be pre-approved by the government and 43% thought that only "completely safe" drugs were allowed to be advertised. Studies conducted by the FDA itself confirm the dangers of DTC advertising. The agency's 2002 survey found that 60% of patients thought that the advertisements provide insufficient information about drug risks and 44% felt similarly about benefits. Fifty-eight percent believed the advertisements made the drugs appear better than they are, and 42% said the advertisements made it seem as if the drug would work for everyone.

Consumer support for these advertisements is actually declining. Compared to a similar FDA survey in 1999, fewer patients responding to the FDA's 2002 survey said that the advertisements had prompted them to talk to a doctor (27% in 1999 vs. 18% in 2002), fewer said that the advertisements provide enough information even to decide whether to consult a physician (70% vs. 58%), fewer felt that the advertisements helped them make better decisions about their own health (47% vs. 32%) and fewer "liked seeing" the advertisements (52% vs. 32%).

Early defenses of DTC advertising asserted that physicians would not be manipulated by patient demands based on DTC advertisements. Unfortunately, this assertion has proved to be wrong. In an already classic study published in the *Journal of the American Medical Association* in April [2005], [R.L.] Kravitz and colleagues sent "standardized patients" with either depression or adjustment disorder into doctors' offices. The patients either 1) described their symptoms and made no specific request for medication; 2) said they had seen a program on television and wondered about drug treatment; or 3) said they had seen a DTC advertisement for Paxil. Of standardized patients with adjustment disorder, a condition not generally requiring drug treatment, 10% of those making no specific request received a prescription (none for Paxil), compared with 55% of those saying they had seen a Paxil advertisement (67% for Paxil) and 39% of those making a general request (26% for Paxil). Clearly these advertisements can spur unnecessary drug prescribing.

General entreaties to physicians [are] actually more effective than those based on DTC advertisements.

Of course, in principle, doctors could be grateful for patients' prompting. But other empirical research suggests otherwise. In one study, doctors were asked whether they considered drugs they had just prescribed to be only "possible" or "unlikely" choices. Fifty percent answered affirmatively for DTC-advertised drugs that were prescribed at the patient's request, compared to only 12% of new prescriptions not requested by patients. Thus, physicians often accede to patients' DTC-driven requests, but are left feeling uneasy.

Price of Health Care Driven Up

Predictably, the cost of health care is being driven up, as patients are induced to request newer, more expensive medications instead of equally effective, older, generic alternatives. One report indicated that the top 25 DTC-advertised drugs accounted for 41% of the growth in retail drug spending in 1999. The report did not separate the effects of DTC advertising from those of advertising to physicians, which often go hand-in-hand. The GAO agreed that "DTC advertising appears to increase prescription drug spending and utilization," primarily because of increased utilization, not increased prices. In a study that did separate out the various forms of advertising, the growth in DTC advertisements for the 25 largest therapeutic classes accounted for 12% of drug sales growth from 1999 to 2000 and resulted in an additional $2.6 billion in pharmaceutical expenditures in 2000. The GAO has estimated that a 10% increase in DTC advertising translates into a 1% increase in sales for that class of drugs, an enormous increase given that many drug classes sell in the billions of dollars. One way or another—through insurance premiums, co-payments or taxes—consumers foot the bill for all this.

The principal benefit asserted by supporters of DTC advertising is that patients with undertreated conditions might receive treatment they otherwise would not have received. This claim remains unproven. The only comprehensive review of studies on DTC advertising concluded that "No empirical research has demonstrated better communication [between patients and physicians] and improved health outcomes." The authors continue: "The onus is on those who might support [DTC advertising] to produce evidence of benefit and, in the absence of this evidence, we must assume that the likely dis-benefits (clinical and economic) outweigh the as yet unproven benefits."

The [pharmaceutical] industry has demonstrated a gross inability to police itself.

Although the review excluded the recent Kravitz study, the Kravitz study hardly supports DTC advertisements. While it is true that, in the Kravitz study, DTC advertisements led to more prescribing of antidepressants for those standardized patients presenting with depression, general entreaties to physicians were actually more effective, than those based on DTC advertisements (76% prescribing rate vs. 53%). (This assumes that prescribing an antidepressant to a depressed patient at his or her first visit is good medicine.) As noted, the study also showed that DTC produced massive overprescribing of antidepressants for those patients with adjustment disorder who have little need for them; the study leaves unanswered whether patients with depression or adjustment disorders are more likely to approach their doctors. Regardless, it seems clear that the purported benefits of DTC advertising can be secured more effectively through noncommercial public-service announcements, without the risk of misleading the public or driving up health-care costs unnecessarily.

FDA Enforcement Is Lackadaisical

For years, Public Citizen has tracked FDA's drug advertising enforcement. . . . Despite a small increase in enforcement activity [in 2005] (and FDA has elsewhere claimed that there has been an increase in enforcement activity for DTC advertising specifically), the broader trend is more important: an 85% decline in enforcement actions between 1998 and 2004, the last year with complete data. Much of this decrease predates the current [George W. Bush] administration, but there was an added drop in 2002. This drop was due to the policy of then-Chief Counsel Daniel Troy to require all regulatory letters to pass through his office, a departure from previous practice and a change that, according to the GAO, "adversely affected" FDA's oversight. The GAO concluded in 2002 that "since the policy change, [the Office of the Chief Counsel's] reviews of draft regulatory letters from FDA have taken so long that misleading advertisements may have completed their broadcast life cycle before FDA issued the letters." According to a report by the Minority Staff of the Committee on Government Reform, in 2003 the average time from initial placement of a prescription drug advertisement and an enforcement action (if any) was 177 days. Recidivism is common; the companies with the largest numbers of advertising-related regulatory letters between 2002 and 2005 were Pfizer (11); Roche, Boehringer Ingelheim and Novartis (five each); and Glaxo (four). The drug advertising division remains greatly understaffed to cope with the continually rising levels of advertising, and DTC advertising in particular.

Even if one were to grant, on a strictly hypothetical basis, that DTC advertisements did, incidentally, convey some useful information to consumers, the real question remains: Are there alternative methods for conveying this information that avoid the risks of DTC advertisements? The answer, as the Kravitz study demonstrates, is an indisputable "yes": If antidepressants were indeed underprescribed, requests based on general entreaties to physicians led to more prescribing than requests based on DTC advertisements. This unproven benefit weighs poorly against the proven risks of DTC advertising.

Protecting the Public

In developing an approach to reducing the harms of DTC advertising, three overriding points are worth noting. First, at least under prevailing legal interpretations, DTC advertising is unlikely to be prohibited in the United States. Second, the industry has demonstrated a gross inability to police itself. It is only the public-relations disaster of the Vioxx debacle that has roused PhRMA [Pharmaceutical Research and Manufacturers of America] to develop DTC advertising guidelines. These guidelines are, of course, voluntary, and are designed primarily to stave off more aggressive legislation or regulation. The guidelines recommend that companies should wait "an appropriate amount of time" after launching a new drug before initiating a DTC campaign. (Senator [Bill] Frist has recommended a two-year waiting period.) Third, the growth of broadcast DTC advertising did not arise magically. Rather, it was the predictable result of FDA's deregulatory efforts.[1] It follows that the genie can, to a large extent, be put back in the bottle.

1. Until 1997, all DTC advertisements that sought to link a disease with a particular drug had to provide the so-called Brief Summary, an often extensive review of potential adverse effects of the drug being advertised. Since 1997, companies have been permitted to refer consumers to websites, print advertisements, or toll-free telephone numbers to obtain this information.

How, then, is the public to be protected from this misleading information? First and foremost, FDA-approved patient information for all prescription drugs is necessary. In 1979, the FDA proposed just this, but opposition from organized medicine, which feared the erosion of its authority, and the pharmaceutical industry ensured that the proposal was withdrawn early in the [Ronald] Reagan administration. In the 1990s, the idea was revisited in the form of FDA-approved Medication Guides, but we estimate that only about 75 drugs of the thousands on the market have such Guides. Instead, the market has been left to the makers of Patient Information Leaflets, which are not FDA-approved and which, as we have shown in three studies, often omit important safety information. FDA-approved information for patients, rather than self-serving advertising, is the appropriate response to the dearth of patient-appropriate drug information. As Franz Ingelfinger, the editor of the *New England Journal of Medicine* once argued, "Advertisements should be overtly recognized for what they are—an unabashed attempt to get someone to buy something, although some useful information may be provided in the process."

Federal agencies could also be doing more to educate patients. The agencies most able to do this are the FDA itself, the National Institutes of Health and the Agency for Healthcare Research and Quality. The failure of these agencies to step into the information gap and fulfill their educational missions allows the industry to cloak its advertising in the mantle of education. Of course, if the industry truly wished to exhort patients to seek care for undertreated medical conditions, it would avail itself only of "help-seeking" advertisements, which inform patients of the existence of particular diseases without naming a treatment. Such advertisements are regulated by the Federal Trade Commission instead of the FDA, presumably because they have less capacity to mislead.

More Regulation of Advertising Needed

Even as DTC advertising has mushroomed from a $791 million industry in 1996 to a $4.1 billion one in 2004, the FDA has yet to publish any regulations regarding DTC advertisements. Some guidances have been promulgated, but these are voluntary and the agency has little ability to enforce them, in part because the advertising division is so severely understaffed and because regulatory letters have to pass through the Office of the Chief Counsel. At a minimum, regulations should provide for pre-review of television advertising and should not allow celebrity endorsements. More fundamentally, the agency still does not have the ability to levy civil monetary penalties. Instead, the FDA issues (often delayed) Warning Letters and Untitled Letters, which often arrive after the advertisement has completed its run, by which time millions of people have already been exposed to their misleading messages.

Health-care observers have long noted that health care is unlike other markets in that patients typically do not purchase services directly. Rather, due to the complexity of the decisions involved and the potentially life-threatening nature of poor choices, the physician acts as a "learned intermediary" on the patient's behalf. DTC advertising is nothing less than an end-run around the doctor-patient relationship—an attempt to turn patients into the agents of pharmaceutical companies as they pressure physicians for medications they may not need.

8

Prescription Drug Advertising Empowers Patients

Paul Antony

Paul Antony is a physician and chief medical officer of Pharmaceutical Research and Manufacturers of America (PhRMA), an organization representing the pharmaceutical industry.

Direct-to-consumer (DTC) advertising helps patients take charge of their own health care by informing them about medical conditions that may afflict them and involving them in the decisions regarding treatment of these conditions. Such advertisements enable patients to identify symptoms of conditions they may be unaware of and examine the available treatment options and the potential side effects of each option. Direct-to-consumer advertising is especially useful in promoting patient-physician dialogue about conditions patients may be reluctant to discuss, such as depression. Claims that DTC advertising has raised the cost of medications are unfounded. In fact, increased use of prescription drugs often leads to decreased spending on more expensive health-care treatments.

DTC Advertising can be a powerful tool in educating millions of people and improving health. Because of DTC advertising, large numbers of Americans are prompted to

Paul Antony, "Hearing on the Impact of Direct-to-Consumer Drug Advertising on Seniors' Health and Health Care Costs," testimony before the Senate Special Committee on Aging, September 29, 2005.

discuss illnesses with their doctors for the first time. Because of DTC advertising, patients become more involved in their own health care decisions, and are proactive in their patient-doctor dialogue. Because of DTC advertising, patients are more likely to take their prescribed medicines. . . .

Informing and Empowering Consumers

Surveys indicate that DTC advertising makes consumers aware of new drugs and their benefits, as well as risks and side effects with the drugs advertised. They help consumers recognize symptoms and seek appropriate care. According to an article in the *New England Journal of Medicine*, DTC advertising is concentrated among a few therapeutic categories. These are therapeutic categories in which consumers can recognize their own symptoms, such as arthritis, seasonal allergies, and obesity; or for pharmaceuticals that treat chronic diseases with many undiagnosed sufferers, such as high cholesterol, osteoporosis, and depression.

DTC advertising gets patients talking to their doctors about conditions that may otherwise have gone undiagnosed or undertreated. For example, a study conducted by RAND Health and published in the *New England Journal of Medicine* found that nearly half of all adults in the United States fail to receive recommended health care. According to researchers on the RAND study, "the deficiencies in care . . . pose serious threats to the health of the American public that could contribute to thousands of preventable deaths in the United States each year." The study found underuse of prescription medications in seven of the nine conditions for which prescription medicines were the recommended treatment. Conditions for which underuse was found include asthma, cerebrovascular disease, congestive heart failure, diabetes, hip fracture, hyperlipidemia and hypertension. Of those seven conditions for which RAND found underuse of recommended prescription medicines, five are DTC advertised.

An FDA survey of physicians ... found that DTC advertisements raise disease awareness and bolster doctor-patient ties.

The RAND Study, as well as other studies, highlight the underuse of needed medications and other healthcare services in the U.S.

- According to a nationally representative study of 9,090 people aged 18 and up, published in *JAMA* [*Journal of the American Medical Association*], about 43 percent of participants with recent major depression are getting inadequate therapy.
- A 2004 study published in the *Archives of Internal Medicine*, found that, "in older patients, failures to prescribe indicated medications, monitor medications appropriately, document necessary information, educate patients, and maintain continuity are more common prescribing problems than is use of inappropriate drugs."
- A May/June 2003 study published in the *Journal of Managed Care Pharmacy*, which examined claims data from 3 of the 10 largest health plans in California to determine the appropriateness of prescription medication use based upon widely accepted treatment guidelines, found that "effective medication appears to be underused." Of the four therapeutic areas of study—asthma CHF [congestive heart failure], depression, and common cold or upper respiratory tract infections—asthma, CHF, and depression were undertreated. The researchers concluded that "the results are particularly surprising and disturbing when we take into account the fact that three of the conditions studied (asthma, CHF, and depression) are known to produce high costs to the healthcare system."

- According to a study released in May 2005 by the Stanford University School of Medicine, among patients with high cholesterol in moderate and high-risk groups, researchers found fewer than half of patient visits ended with a statin [drug designed to lower cholesterol] recommendation. Based on the findings, the researchers say physicians should be more aggressive in investigating statin therapy for patients with a high or moderate risk of heart disease, and that patients should ask for their cholesterol levels to be checked regularly.

Increasing Communication Between Doctor and Patient

A vast majority of patients (93 percent) who asked about a drug reported that their doctor "welcomed the questions" [according to a study by K. Aikin and J. Swazy]. Of patients who asked about a drug, 77 percent reported that their relationship with their doctor remained unchanged as a result of the office visit, and 20 percent reported that their relationship improved. In addition, both an FDA [Food and Drug Administration] survey of physicians (from a random sample of 500 physicians from the American Medical Association's database) and a survey by the nation's oldest and largest African-American medical association, found that DTC advertisements raise disease awareness and bolster doctor-patient ties.

The doctor-patient relationship is enhanced if DTC advertising prompts a patient to talk to his doctor for the first time about a previously undiscussed condition, to comply with a prescribed treatment regimen, or to become aware of a risk or side effect that was otherwise unknown. A 2002 *Prevention Magazine* survey found that 24.8 million Americans spoke with their doctor about a medical condition for the first time as a result of seeing a DTC advertisement. Similarly, the FDA patient survey on DTC advertising found that nearly one in five patients reported speaking to a physician about a condition for the first time because of a DTC ad.

PhRMA and its member companies believe it is vital that patients, in consultation with their doctors, make decisions about treatments and medicines. Prescribing decisions should be dominated by the doctor's advice. While our member companies direct a large majority of their promotional activities toward physicians, such promotion in no way guarantees medicines will be prescribed.

According to reports and studies, there is no direct relationship between DTC advertising and the price growth of drugs.

According to a General Accounting Office report, of the 61.1 million people (33 percent of adults) who had discussions with their physician as a result of a DTC advertisement in 2001, only 8.5 million (5 percent of adults) actually received a prescription for the product, a small percentage of the total volume of prescriptions dispensed. Indeed, an FDA survey of physicians revealed that the vast majority of physicians do not feel pressure to prescribe. According to the survey, 91 percent of physicians said that their patients did not try to influence treatment courses in a way that would have been harmful, and 72 percent of physicians, when asked for a prescription for a specific brand name drug, felt little or no pressure to prescribe a medicine.

DTC advertising also encourages patients to discuss medical problems that otherwise may not have been discussed because it was either thought to be too personal or that there was a stigma attached to the disease. For example, a *Health Affairs* article examined the value of innovation and noted that depression medications, known as selective serotonin reuptake inhibitors (SSRIs), that have been DTC advertised, have led to significant treatment expansion. Prior to the 1990's, it was estimated that about half of those persons who met a clinical definition of depression were not appropriately diagnosed, and many of those diagnosed did not receive clinically appropriate treatment. However, in the 1990's with the advent of SSRIs, treatment has been expanded. According to the article, "Manufacturers of SSRIs encouraged doctors to watch for depression and the reduced stigma afforded by the new medications induced patients to seek help." As a result, diagnosis and treatment for depression doubled over the 1990's.

Pharmaceutical Utilization and DTC Advertising

According to reports and studies, there is no direct relationship between DTC advertising and the price growth of drugs. For example, in comments to the FDA in December 2003, the FTC [Federal Trade Commission] stated, "[DTC advertising] can empower consumers to manage their own health care by providing information that will help them, with the assistance of their doctors, to make better informed decisions about their treatment options. ... Consumers receive these benefits from DTC advertising with little, if any, evidence that such advertising increases prescription drug prices." Notably, since January 2000, the CPI [Consumer Price Index] component that tracks prescription medicines has been in line with overall medical inflation.

The FTC comments referenced above also note, "DTC advertising accounts for a relatively small proportion of the total cost of drugs, which reinforces the view that such advertising would have a limited, if any, effect on price." Likewise, a study by Harvard University and the Massachusetts Institute of Technology and published by the Kaiser Family Foundation found that DTC advertising accounts for less than 2 percent of the total U.S. spending for prescription medicines.

One study in the *American Journal of Managed Care* looked at whether pharmaceutical marketing has led to an increase in the use of medications by patients with marginal indications. The study found that high-risk individuals were receiving lipid-lowering treatment "consistent with evidence-based practice guidelines" despite the fact that "a substantial portion of patients continue to remain untreated and undertreated. ...." The study concluded that "greater overall use did not appear to be associated with a shift towards patients with less CV [cardiovascular] risk."

Increased spending on pharmaceuticals often leads to lower spending on other forms of more costly health care.

Pharmaceutical utilization is increasing for reasons other than DTC advertising. As the June 2003 study of DTC advertising [DTCA] commissioned by the Kaiser Family Foundation found, "[O]ur estimates indicate that DTCA is important, but not the primary driver of recent growth [in prescription drug spending]."

Other reasons pharmaceutical utilization is increasing, include:

- **Improved Medicines** —Many new medicines replace higher-cost surgeries and hospital care. In 2004 alone, pharmaceutical companies added 38 new medicines, and over the last decade, over 300 new medicines have become available for treating patients. These include important new medicines for some of the most devastating and costly diseases, including: AIDS, cancer, heart disease, Alzheimer's, and diabetes. According to a study prepared for the Department of Health and Human Services, "[n]ew medications are not simply more costly than older ones. They may be more effective or have fewer side effects; some may treat conditions for which no treatment was available."

- **New Standards of Medical Practice Encouraging Greater Use of Pharmaceuticals** —Clinical standards are changing to emphasize earlier and tighter control of a range of conditions, such as diabetes, hypertension and cardiovascular disease. For example, new recommendations from the two provider groups suggest that early treatment, including lifestyle changes and *treatment with two or more types of medications*, can significantly reduce the risk of later complications and improve the quality of life for people with type 2 diabetes.

- **Greater Treatment of Previously Undiagnosed and Untreated Conditions** —According to guidelines developed by the National Heart, Lung, and Blood Institute's National Cholesterol Education Program (NCEP) Adult Treatment Panel (ATP), approximately 36 million adults should be taking medicines to lower their cholesterol, a number that has grown from 13 million just 8 years ago [in 1997].

- **Aging of America** —The aging of America translates into greater reliance on pharmaceuticals. For example, congestive heart failure affects an estimated 2 percent of Americans age 40 to 59, more than 5 percent of those aged 60 to 69, and 10 percent of those 70 or more.

While some assume that DTC advertising leads to increased use of newer medicines rather than generic medicines, generics represent just over 50 percent of all prescriptions (generics are historically not DTC advertised). In contrast, in Europe, where DTC advertising is prohibited, the percentage of prescriptions that are generic is significantly lower. Likewise, it is worth noting that while broadcast DTC has been in place since 1997, the rate of growth in drug cost increases has declined in each of the last 5 years [2000–2004] and in 2004 was below the rate of growth in overall health care costs.

Economic Value of DTC Advertising

Increased spending on pharmaceuticals often leads to lower spending on other forms of more costly health care. New drugs are the most heavily advertised drugs, a point critics often emphasize. However, the use of newer drugs tends to lower all types of non-drug medical spending, resulting in a net reduction in the total cost of treating a condition. For example, on average replacing an older drug with a drug 15 years newer increases spending on drugs by $18, but reduces overall costs by $111.

The Tufts Center for the Study of Drug Development reports that disease management organizations surveyed believe that increased spending on prescription drugs reduces hospital in-patient costs. "Since prescription drugs account for less than 10 percent of total current U.S. health care spending, while in-patient care accounts for 32 percent, the increased use of appropriate pharmaceutical therapies may help moderate or reduce growth in the costliest component of the U.S. health care system," according to Tufts Center Director Kenneth I. Kaitin.

Opponents also compare the amount of money spent by drug companies on marketing and advertising to the amount they spend on research and development of new drugs. However, in 2004, pharmaceutical manufacturers spent an estimated $4.15 billion on DTC advertising, according to IMS Health, compared to $49.3 billion in total R&D [research and development] spending by the biopharmaceutical industry, according to Burrill & Company. PhRMA members alone spent $38.8 billion on R&D in 2004.

DTC advertising provides value to patients by making them aware of risks and benefits of new drugs; it empowers patients and enhances the public health; it plays a vital role in addressing a major problem in this country of undertreatment and underdiagnosis of disease; encourages patients to discuss medical problems with their health care provider that may otherwise not be discussed due to a stigma being attached to the disease; and encourages patient compliance with physician-directed treatment regimens.

Given the progress that continues to be made in society's battle against disease, patients are seeking more information about medical problems and potential treatments. The purpose of DTC advertising is to foster an informed conversation about health, disease and treatments between patients and their health care practitioners.

9

Low-Income Americans Are Undermedicated

Marie C. Reed

Marie C. Reed is a data manager for the Center for Studying Health System Change, a policy research organization focused on the American health-care system.

According to a household survey conducted by the Center for Studying Health System Change (HSC), the number of Americans reporting difficulty affording prescription medications increased by at least 12 percent between 2001 and 2003. Because prescription drug use in the United States has risen dramatically in the past decade, many health plans have increased their out-of-pocket payment requirements for prescriptions. In addition, many low-income people with chronic conditions and older people devote large portions of their incomes to medical bills, leaving little money for prescribed drugs. In addition, the survey also showed that consumers who have no insurance or are covered by public insurance such as Medicaid have greater problems getting access to prescription drugs than those who are privately insured. While the Medicare prescription drug benefit that became effective in 2006 will help many older people, and private drug discount plans provide relief to other segments of the population, the number of low-income Americans who cannot afford prescription drugs will continue to grow.

Marie C. Reed, from a study for Studying Health Care System Change, 2005. Reprinted with permission of the Center for Studying Health System Change, Washington D.C. www.hschange.org.

The proportion of American adults reporting problems affording prescription drugs ticked up between 2001 and 2003, increasing from 12.0 percent to 12.8 percent, according to HSC's nationally representative Household Survey. This small but statistically significant increase in affordability problems likely resulted from higher prescribing rates and increased patient cost sharing.

Among all adults, prescription drug access problems rose markedly for adults with chronic conditions, increasing from 16.5 percent in 2001 to 18.3 percent in 2003. However, access problems for adults without chronic conditions remained unchanged at about 9.2 percent during the same period. People with chronic conditions are more likely to need prescription drugs to manage their conditions, prevent complications and maintain quality of life. Partly because of higher prescription drug needs, adults living with chronic conditions in 2003 were twice as likely as those without chronic conditions to be unable to afford all of their prescription drugs.

Between 2001 and 2003, the proportion of privately insured working-age adults (aged 18–64) with chronic health conditions who didn't purchase all of their prescriptions because of cost concerns increased from 12.7 percent to 15.2 percent. In the past decade, prescription drug utilization and spending in the United States increased dramatically. In an effort to control rising prescription drug spending, health plans started using formularies more aggressively and increasing patients' out-of-pocket payment requirements. These policies likely are a key reason for the increase in prescription drug access problems for privately insured working-age Americans with chronic conditions.

Insurance Disparities

Cost-related unmet prescription drug needs did not increase for working-age adults with chronic conditions who are uninsured or who are covered by public insurance, such as Medicaid. However, uninsured and publicly insured working-age adults with chronic conditions continue to have significantly higher rates of access problems than the privately insured. In 2003, one in two uninsured, nearly one in three publicly insured and one in six privately insured working-age adults with at least one chronic condition didn't purchase all of their prescription drugs because of cost concerns.

While unmet needs for prescription drugs for privately insured people are relatively low, the privately insured constitute a sizeable segment of the overall population that reports problems affording prescription drugs. In 2003, 40 percent of adults with chronic conditions who reported prescription drug affordability problems were working age and privately insured—more than 5.5 million people.

Low-income, uninsured working-age adults with chronic conditions were most likely to have cost-related [prescription drug] access problems.

Elderly Medicare beneficiaries living with chronic conditions who had private supplemental coverage—employer-sponsored or Medigap—were not more likely to report problems affording their prescriptions in 2003 than in 2001. But prescription drug access problems did increase for beneficiaries lacking supplemental private coverage, growing from 12.4 percent in 2001 to 16.4 percent in 2003. Many without private insurance did not have access to discounted prescription drug prices, a feature of many supplemental plans, and often had to pay list price.

Income and Rx Access

Regardless of insurance coverage, low-income adults—those with incomes below 200 percent of the federal poverty level, or $36,800 for a family of four in 2003—with chronic conditions faced significant financial barriers to obtaining prescribed drugs.

Low-income, uninsured working-age adults with chronic conditions were most likely to have cost-related access problems, with nearly 60 percent reporting they could not afford all their prescriptions in 2003. . . . Nearly 40 percent of chronically ill low-income people with public insurance, such as Medicaid, were unable to fill at least one prescription because of cost concerns. And, in 2003, the rate of access problems for low-income, privately insured working-age adults with chronic conditions was similar to that faced by those with public insurance—nearly 35 percent had cost-related unmet prescription drug needs. Among low-income elderly Medicare beneficiaries, 17 percent reported being unable to fill at least one prescription.

Many low-income people with chronic conditions who can't afford prescription drugs face substantial medical bills. Regardless of insurance coverage, about half of low-income working-age adults with chronic conditions and an unmet prescription drug need paid more than 5 percent of their incomes for medical expenses in 2003. And more than half of these—nearly 1.8 million working-age adults—paid more than 10 percent of their incomes for medical expenses and still were unable to purchase all of their prescriptions. These estimates are conservative since payments for insurance premiums were not included as out-of-pocket medical expenses.

Likewise, many older people are paying significant portions of their income for medical care and still can't afford all of their prescriptions. In 2003, for example, 56 percent of the elderly with low incomes and chronic conditions who couldn't afford all their prescriptions spent at least 5 percent of their income on medical care, and 37 percent paid more than 10 percent.

Blacks at Higher Risk

Privately insured working-age blacks with chronic conditions were nearly twice as likely as whites to not be able to afford all of their prescriptions—22 percent vs. 13 percent—in 2003. Similarly, 17 percent of black elderly Medicare beneficiaries reported problems affording prescription drugs compared with 9 percent of white beneficiaries. Between 2001 and 2003, cost-related prescription drug access disparities for blacks compared with whites did not change. Previous HSC research found that, in 2001, working-age black Americans with private insurance and elderly black Medicare beneficiaries were much more likely than comparable white Americans to have cost-related unmet prescription drug needs and that these disparities remained after adjusting for income and other socioeconomic factors.

More than 14 million American adults of all ages with chronic conditions . . . could not afford all of their prescriptions in 2003.

This type of racial disparity does not exist to a significant extent between uninsured or publicly insured blacks and whites with chronic conditions—their prescription access problems are high regardless of race. For example, nearly one in three working-age chronically ill whites and blacks with public insurance reported not being able to afford a prescription drug, while 53 percent of uninsured whites and 60 percent of uninsured blacks couldn't afford to fill a prescription.

African-Americans are more likely to have certain chronic conditions, such as hypertension and diabetes, than whites. This double jeopardy—a combination of higher disease rates and greater inability to afford all prescriptions—results in much higher overall risk for blacks compared with whites. For example, 7 percent of all working-age black Americans had hypertension in 2003 and were unable to purchase all of their prescriptions because of cost concerns—nearly three times the rate for working-age whites.

Implications for the Future

More than 14 million American adults of all ages with chronic conditions—more than half with low incomes—could not afford all of their prescriptions in 2003. One-fifth of adults with chronic conditions who had cost-related unmet prescription drug needs in 2003 were elderly, one-fifth were uninsured, a fifth had public insurance, such as Medicaid, and two-fifths were privately insured.

Many older people will be helped by the Medicare prescription drug benefit that goes into effect in 2006, but other significant segments of the American public also are unable to afford all of their prescriptions. Some of the uninsured may be helped by private drug discount plans. For example, the U.S. Department of Health and Human Services recently announced the Together Rx Access Card, a prescription drug discount plan sponsored by 10 pharmaceutical companies that may help uninsured persons save up to 40 percent on some prescriptions. While this effort is likely to increase the affordability of prescription drugs for many people, some uninsured people, especially those with low incomes, would still face significant out-of-pocket costs for prescription drugs.

As states wrestle with budget problems, Americans who rely on Medicaid for access to prescription drugs are likely to experience more affordability problems. Many states are instituting additional cost-containment policies to control the growth of prescription drug spending, including limiting the number of allowable prescriptions and requiring patients to pay a portion of the cost.

Since 2002, employers and private health plans have shifted costs to workers through increased patient cost sharing, especially for prescription drugs. This trend continued in 2003 and 2004, and it is unclear where employers will draw the line on increased patient cost sharing.

As medical needs for prescription drugs continue to grow, it's likely that the proportion of working-age Americans, especially those with chronic conditions, going without prescription drugs because of cost concerns will continue to grow.

10

Americans with Chronic Pain Are Undermedicated

Barry Yeoman

Barry Yeoman is a journalist whose work has appeared in the New York Times, Discover, Mother Jones, O: The Oprah Magazine, Reader's Digest, *and other publications. He is a contributing editor to* AARP: The Magazine.

Approximately 75 million Americans are victims of chronic pain, according to the American Medical Association, and these patients often do not receive the medication that could provide them relief. Although doctors know how to treat pain, they are often reluctant to prescribe pain medication, particularly opioids such as morphine and oxycodone, because such medications can lead to addiction. Some doctors also fear facing prosecution by the federal Drug Enforcement Administration or state medical boards for prescribing large amounts of such drugs. Finally, some hospitals are beginning to take chronic pain seriously, creating programs specifically dealing with pain management. Moreover, doctors who neglect their patients' cries for pain relief have even faced legal repercussions in recent years. Still, some patients themselves harbor misconceptions and reject pain medication even when it is offered, despite research that shows the low risk of addiction.

Barry Yeoman, "Prisoners of Pain," *AARP Magazine*, September–October 2005. Copyright 1995–2003, AARP. Reproduced by permission of the author.

Deborah Hamalainen was feeling more and more agitated by the minute. Waiting to see her neurologist, she was silently rehearsing a confrontation that had been building for months. She planned to look the doctor directly in the eyes and demand that he treat the chronic pain that had invaded her life.

In the two decades since doctors diagnosed her with multiple sclerosis, Hamalainen learned to tolerate numb extremities, tingling sensations, even the weakness that causes her left foot to drag. And it wasn't like her to be confrontational. "I'm much happier in denial," admits the soft-spoken 52-year-old sculptor.

The symptoms she couldn't ignore, though, were the intense shooting pains that raced across her shoulder blades and down her limbs. By the time she arrived for this doctor's appointment, they were a 24-hour presence. Hamalainen barely slept anymore. Rolling over was an ordeal. When the Medford, New Jersey, resident awoke, stiff and exhausted, she braced her shoulders so they wouldn't move as she rose. Sometimes, her husband had to pull her upright from the bed.

Every three months for three years, Hamalainen saw this neurologist. Each time, she mentioned the pain. Each time, the doctor deftly changed the subject. Each time, she left in pain.

But this time would be different. Hamalainen waited quietly as nurses wandered in and out of the examination room, taking her vital signs. Finally, she lost it. "My pain is real," she said frantically to one of the nurses. "I need relief. Why does he keep refusing to talk to me about it? What do I have to do?"

The nurse turned to her conspiratorially and lowered her voice. "I should not tell you this," she said. "But he doesn't want to treat your pain because the treatment that works is opioids, and he's afraid to prescribe them." With that conversation, Hamalainen joined legions of patients who are the victims of a troubling and all-too-common medical practice: the undertreatment of significant and debilitating pain. An estimated 75 million Americans suffer from chronic pain, according to the American Medical Association, and numerous studies have shown that patients often don't receive the medication that could provide relief. Undertreatment runs as high as 50 percent among advanced-stage cancer patients and 85 percent among older Americans living in long-term care facilities.

Many [doctors] harbor the false impression that opioids frequently lead to addiction.

Doctors Are Afraid to Prescribe

Much of this suffering is preventable. Experts do know how to reduce pain safely. In particular, physicians now know that opioid analgesics—medicines such as morphine and oxycodone—provide relief for a wide spectrum of pain problems, with relatively few side effects when taken as prescribed. "We can't cure everybody who is in pain, but we can make almost everyone feel better," says Scott Fishman, chief of the division of pain medicine at the University of California [UC], Davis, and president of the American Academy of Pain Medicine. "Becoming a prisoner of pain is not an inevitability."

The problem is that the most effective medications cause skittishness among many physicians. Poor medical-school training has left them unaware of the tools at their disposal and even the importance of treating pain. Many harbor the false impression that opioids frequently lead to addiction or unmanageable side effects, even when used correctly for a legitimate medical need.

Worse, some physicians fear that if they deliver humane pain care, they'll face prosecution by the federal Drug Enforcement Administration (DEA) or state medical boards. In recent years, a number of respected doctors have been investigated and even prosecuted after prescribing large amounts of opioids. The result, according to experts, is an environment that scares doctors away from practicing good medicine.

"I've had prominent physicians call me up and say, 'I have patients doing well, taking opioids for otherwise treatable pain, but I'm going to stop writing prescriptions because I don't want the DEA coming into my office and putting handcuffs on me,'" says James Campbell, a neurosurgeon at Johns Hopkins University. "Five years ago, we were actually doing a better job at handling pain patients. Now we've seen a backslide, and patients are definitely the victims. They're suffering."

Pain Is a Disease

On his first day as a licensed physician, Russell Portenoy had a troubling experience that would influence the course of his career. At the New York City hospital where he was interning, a nurse summoned him to a room where a cancer patient was moaning with abdominal pain. Portenoy knew the woman would benefit from opioids, but he was new at doctoring, so he first phoned the resident in charge to clear his decision.

"I have a patient here. She's 60 years old, she's got metastatic ovarian cancer, and she's in bad pain," Portenoy told his supervisor.

"What do you want to do?" the resident asked.

"Well, I thought we should give her some pain medicine."

"What do you want to give her?"

"Morphine."

There was silence on the other end of the line. It was 1980: even physicians who endorsed opioids for terminally ill patients believed that morphine was too potent and too dangerous. Finally, the resident said, "Look, you're the doctor. You want to give her morphine, give her morphine." After further consultation, Portenoy wrote an order for a 3 mg injection, less than one third of what he would likely give her today. He never checked back to see if the medication worked.

The patient was still on Portenoy's mind the following year when he decided to specialize in pain medicine. "I'd given somebody with severe cancer pain a dose that didn't have a prayer of providing any benefit," he says. "My hope is that there was such a profound placebo effect that she didn't scream the rest of the night."

Portenoy joined a coterie of pioneers who encouraged their colleagues to become bolder in treating patients' suffering. They argued that pain is more than a symptom; it's a disease by itself that can trigger a cascade of other health problems—from a weakened immune system to obesity—if left untended.

At Memorial Sloan-Kettering Cancer Center, where he launched his career as a researcher and pain physician, Portenoy initially concentrated on cancer pain. Eventually he discovered that opioid medicines—routinely prescribed in advanced-cancer cases—also worked for patients without terminal illnesses. They relieved the symptoms without fogging patients' brains or turning them into addicts. The only major ongoing side effect, constipation, was manageable with other drugs. But when Portenoy shared the news in a 1986 journal article, he received excoriating criticism from his colleagues.

Slowly, time has proven Portenoy correct. In 1996 two leading professional groups declared opioids "an essential part of a pain-management plan." Five years later, the DEA and 21 health organizations agreed that opioids are often "the most effective way to treat pain and often the only treatment option that provides significant relief."

Across the United States, hospitals are starting to take the issue seriously, creating programs specializing in pain management. Portenoy's own department, at New York City's Beth

Israel Medical Center, has 14 physicians, a team of researchers, and training programs for doctors and others. Using opioids and other therapies, these programs have restored normalcy to many lives.

Millions of Americans still don't receive the therapy they need.

"It's a miracle," says 55-year-old Michele Ferreri, a Staten Island, New York, woman who suffers from a painful nerve condition that appeared in the aftermath of shingles. Once unable to get out of bed because of her burning headaches, she started taking extended-release morphine and other medications after seeing Portenoy at Beth Israel. Now she lives an active life, taking her mother shopping, doing laundry, and attending social functions with her husband, a hospital CEO [chief executive officer]. "I can smile now," she says. "I can smile and greet people."

Widely Held Misconceptions

Until recently, there was no legal incentive for doctors to take pain seriously. That's starting to change. In 2001 a California jury awarded $1.5 million to the family of a lung-cancer patient who lay undermedicated and dying in a hospital near San Francisco. (The award was later reduced in keeping with state law.) Two years later, the California Medical Board reprimanded a physician in a similar case involving a nursing home. These decisions "sound a resounding wake-up call to all health care providers that failure to treat pain attentively will result in accountability," says Kathryn Tucker, attorney for Compassion & Choices, which litigated the cases.

But the wake-up call hasn't stirred everyone. Millions of Americans still don't receive the therapy they need. "The odds of your getting good pain management are, at best, 50-50," says UC Davis bioethicist Ben Rich.

Studies bear Rich out. One survey of Oregon families, published in 2004, showed that almost half of terminally ill patients were in significant pain or distress during the last week of their lives. In a study of nursing homes in 11 states, Brown University researchers found that two thirds of the residents initially found to be in daily pain were still suffering two to six months later.

But even when treatment is available, patients often reject it because of widely held misconceptions. Popular media play up addiction—be it on the TV series *ER*, where Noah Wyle portrayed a young physician addicted to prescription painkillers, or in tabloid newspapers, which devoted voluminous ink to [talk show host] Rush Limbaugh's struggle with pain pills in late 2003. Indeed, Limbaugh's alleged drug of choice, Oxy-Contin (a form of oxycodone), has become popular among rural drug abusers, who chew the pills to destroy their time-release mechanism and get a heroinlike rush.

In reality, for those using opioids as prescribed, the likelihood of addiction is extremely low, according to research. "It's really an unwarranted fear," says Christine Miaskowski, former president of the American Pain Society. Many patients do become physiologically dependent—meaning they'd go through withdrawal syndrome if they quit cold turkey—but this is a normal condition that can be managed by tapering down the dosage. It's not the same as addiction, which requires psychological dependence. Experts say patients with a history of drug abuse can safely use opioids too, as long as they are carefully monitored by their physicians to avoid a recurrence of their abusive behaviors.

These reassurances don't convince everyone. "There is a just-say-no-to-drugs attitude in the United States," says Diane Meier, a geriatric and palliative-care specialist at New York City's Mount Sinai Medical Center. "Even my own family will say, 'I don't want to be doped up on those drugs.'"

Patients aren't alone in their misinformation. Physicians, trained to suspect there's an abuser lurking behind every painkiller request—and, to be fair, there sometimes is—still confuse addiction with physical dependence. The facts don't dissuade them: although Ferreri has become functional on morphine, her family doctor still "talks to my husband all the time about the amount of medication I'm on, how dangerous it is. He really makes me feel that I'm a drug addict."

Worse, some physicians simply don't understand the importance of treating pain at all. Miaskowski, a professor in the physiological nursing department at the University of California, San Francisco, recently completed a study of cancer patients. "We had one patient whose primary care physician told her, 'Don't take your pain medicine. Let the pain kill the cancer.'" Was this advice offered years before recent advances in pain management? No, she says. "This was 2001."

Drug Diversion

There's another, more ominous reason some doctors don't treat pain aggressively: they don't want to end up like Arizona physician Jeri Hassman.

Hassman, a physical medicine and rehabilitation specialist licensed in 1986, opened a solo practice in 1999 to focus on nonsurgical treatments for injured patients. Working with physical therapists and chiropractors, she developed a comprehensive program that includes massage, electrical stimulation, muscle injections, and even posture lessons. She also prescribed painkillers. "Medications are important," she says. "If you decrease pain, you get better compliance with exercise and other rehabilitation." Until 2002, she says, "I wasn't afraid of prescribing strong pain medicines alongside the available therapies."

Then, in May of that year, federal agents stormed her Tucson office in full view of her patients. They spent eight hours questioning her staff, seizing patient files and appointment logs, and copying the hard drives off her computers. According to a government brief, the DEA had been contacted by pharmacists "concerned about the large amounts of narcotic drugs that were being prescribed for Dr. Hassman's patients, plus the frequency with which they were returning for refills." The druggists were also concerned that some medicines had fallen into the hands of nonpatients, the brief said. Hassman was arrested and charged with 320 counts of illegally distributing narcotics and 41 counts of health care fraud.

Physician groups and patient advocates point to a growing list of respected pain doctors who have been prosecuted [for prescribing pain killers].

Just before the case was scheduled for trial, federal prosecutors offered Hassman a plea agreement, allowing her to plead guilty to four counts of failing to report prescription abuse. Unwilling to risk a jury trial, Hassman accepted the offer. She was sentenced to two years' probation and agreed to surrender her DEA license to prescribe controlled substances.

Hassman was relatively lucky. [In 2005], Virginia pain specialist William Hurwitz was sentenced to 25 years in prison for drug trafficking after prescribing large doses of painkillers such as OxyContin, morphine, and methadone to his patients. One of his patients died after taking a very high dose of morphine. DEA officials likened Hurwitz to a heroin dealer. Others, though, testified that Hurwitz provided them with the only effective relief they had ever received for debilitating pain.

Though the DEA wouldn't comment for this article, it has previously insisted that it only goes after bad apples. "Our focus is not on pain doctors. Our focus is on people who divert drugs," agency official Patricia Good said during a 2004 teleconference. But physician groups and patient advocates point to a growing list of respected pain doctors who have been prosecuted by the DEA and by state medical boards. They say that while the DEA has a legitimate interest in preventing the diversion of harmful drugs, the agency's adversarial zeal has grown in the past four or five years.

For its part, the DEA notes that it arrests fewer than 100 doctors a year on drug-diversion charges—hardly a full-scale attack on the profession. The numbers hardly matter, though, because the arrests, and the publicity surrounding them, have created a chilling effect. "Every time a physician picks up a newspaper or hears an account of some physician who has been accused of inappropriately prescribing controlled substances, it reinforces the proposition [that] bad things can happen to you when you attempt to manage patients' pain aggressively but appropriately," says bioethicist Ben Rich. "Doctors don't say, 'I'll be more judicious and that won't happen to me.' Their reaction is, 'I don't need this.'"

A New Life

It took Deborah Hamalainen another year, plus the encouragement of a friend, to find effective treatment for her pain. Early one morning, the two women took an 80-mile bus trip to New York City, then took a taxi downtown to Beth Israel Medical Center. There, Hamalainen met with pain specialist Russell Portenoy, who found her story credible. Portenoy explained to Hamalainen that he couldn't cure her multiple sclerosis, but he could control her symptoms. "The goal is to focus on the pain itself, to get you comfortable, and to help you function," he told her.

After monitoring several medications for side effects, Portenoy and Hamalainen settled on fentanyl, a synthetic opioid delivered through an adhesive patch worn on her lower back. She uses oxycodone as a "rescue" drug when the fentanyl isn't effective.

As Portenoy predicted, the medicine hasn't eliminated the source of Hamalainen's pain. In fact, the multiple sclerosis has progressed. She's been losing feeling in her hands and feet, dropping objects, and tripping. She relies on a pair of canes to get around. Still, with the pain under control, Hamalainen has been able to return to her art. She recently had a mixed-media exhibition at the gallery where she used to work. In one sculpture, she took old canes—including the ones her father used after he lost a leg to diabetes—and smashed them with an ax, then enclosed them in a clear plastic exhibition box.

When the pain was at its worst, Hamalainen contemplated suicide. Now, with opioids to relieve the symptoms, Hamalainen can envision a productive artistic future. "Being able to be creative again has been thrilling," she says. "It's like having a new life."

11

Overmedication Causes Health Problems for Many Elderly Americans

Cynthia M. Williams

Cynthia M. Williams is assistant professor of family medicine at Uniformed Services University of the Health Sciences in Bethesda, Maryland. She completed her residency at Naval Hospital at Camp Pendleton, California, and a geriatric fellowship at East Carolina University School of Medicine in Greenville, North Carolina.

As the U.S. elderly population grows, so does the consumption of prescription drugs, since older patients consume about 30 percent of all such drugs. While some of these drugs help with the chronic medical problems of the aging population, overmedication is a serious problem that can cause additional health problems. For example, polypharmacy, the simultaneous use of several medications, can be harmful, especially if a patient is prescribed a medication at too high a dose or for too long. The main danger of polypharmacy is adverse drug interactions. Doctors must therefore be watchful to prevent the hazards of multiple prescriptions. In addition, many elderly people suffer adverse drug reactions because they are prescribed drugs that are not appropriate for older persons, especially those who are frail. To address this problem, experts have developed a list of potentially inappropri-

Cynthia M. Williams, "Using Medications Properly in Older Adults," *American Family Physician*, v. 66, November 15, 2002. Copyright © 2002 American Academy of Family Physicians. Reproduced by permission.

ate drugs for older people that physicians should refer to when treating the elderly. To reduce the problem of overmedication, physicians also need to evaluate elderly patients' prescriptions on each visit.

The U.S. population is aging. Patients 65 years and older represent approximately 13 percent of the population, but they consume about 30 percent of all prescription medications. Older American consumers spend an average total of $3 billion annually on prescription medications. Sixty-one percent of older people seeing a physician are taking at least one prescription medication, and most older Americans take an average of three to five medications. These data do not include the use of over-the-counter medications or herbal therapies. An estimated 40 percent of older Americans have used some form of dietary supplement within the past year.

The physician who cares for aging patients with numerous chronic medical conditions must make daily decisions about appropriate drug therapy. More than 60 percent of all physician visits include a prescription for medication. The multiple medications and complex drug schedules may be justified for older persons with complex medical problems. However, the use of too many medications can pose problems of serious adverse drug events and drug-drug interactions, and often can contribute to nonadherence.

Problems with Drug Therapy

Many factors influence the efficacy, safety, and success of drug therapy with older patients. These factors include not only the effects of aging on the pharmacokinetics [how the body interacts with a drug] and pharmacodynamics [a drug's action] of medications but also patient characteristics and other issues, including atypical presentation of illness, the use of multiple health care professionals, and adherence to drug regimens.

Adherence or compliance with drug therapy is essential to successful medical management. Noncompliance or nonadherence with drug therapy in older patient populations ranges from 21 to 55 percent. The reasons for nonadherence include more medication use (total number of pills taken per day), forgetting or confusion about dosage schedule, intentional nonadherence because of medication side effects, and increased sensitivity to drugs leading to toxicity and adverse events. Older patients may intentionally take too much of a medication, thinking it will help speed their recovery, while others, who cannot afford the medications, may undermedicate or simply not take any of the medication. Simple interventions by the health care team, such as reinforcing the importance of taking the prescribed dose and encouraging use of pill calendar boxes, can improve adherence and overall compliance with drug therapy.

Drug-induced adverse events can mimic other geriatric syndromes . . . causing the physician to prescribe yet another drug.

Adverse Drug Events

One study revealed that adverse drug events in older patients led to hospitalizations in 25 percent of patients 80 years and older. Adverse drug reactions are a common cause of iatrogenic illness [illness inadvertently induced by medical treatment] in this age group, with psychotropic [mood-altering] and cardiovascular drugs accounting for many of these. Many drugs can cause distressing and potentially disabling or life-threatening reactions. . . .

Polypharmacy is simply the use of many medications at the same time. Other definitions include prescribing more medication than is clinically indicated, a medical regimen that includes at least one unnecessary medication, or the empiric use of five or more medications. Polypharmacy is particularly harmful when the patient receives too many medications for too long and in too high a dosage. The major concern about polypharmacy is the potential for adverse drug reactions and interactions. It has been estimated that for every dollar spent on pharmaceuticals in nursing homes, another dollar is spent treating the iatrogenic illnesses attributed to the medications. Drug-induced adverse events can mimic other geriatric syndromes or precipitate confusion, falls, and incontinence, possibly causing the physician to prescribe yet another drug. This prescribing cascade is a preventable problem that requires the physician to be certain that all medications being taken by the patient are appropriately indicated, safe, and effective. . . .

Avoiding Harmful Drug Reactions

Drug-related problems including therapeutic failure, adverse drug reactions, and adverse drug withdrawal events are common in older patients. To address this problem, a list of drugs that may be inappropriate to prescribe to older persons, especially the frail elderly, was developed through a consensus of experts in geriatric medicine and pharmacology. This list, known as the Beers criteria, was originally targeted at nursing homes but has been expanded for community-dwelling seniors.

Prescribing medications for older adults requires maintaining a balance between using too few and too little, and too many and too much.

A recent review of the Beers criteria applied to various health care settings, from community-dwelling seniors to frail nursing home patients, found that between one in four and one in seven older patients received at least one inappropriate medication. The problematic drugs most often prescribed were long-acting benzodiazepines, dipyridamole (Persantine), propoxyphene (Darvon), and amitriptyline (Elavil). When applying these criteria to a patient, it is important to remember that if a drug has been used for a long time without a serious adverse effect, it may not need to be discontinued. The physician should continually monitor a patient's drug list and carefully ascertain if any medication is causing harm. Physicians can address this issue by keeping a list of drugs that can cause serious adverse events when prescribed to older adults. . . .

To avoid adverse drug events and polypharmacy, drugs that are beneficial in the treatment or prevention of serious diseases may not be prescribed to older adults. For example, clinical evidence is now available showing that older adults benefit from beta-blocker therapy after myocardial infarction [heart attack], adequate control of hypertension [high blood pressure], and adequate treatment of hyperlipidemia [high cholesterol and other fats in the blood]. Other medications that have shown benefit in older adults, but are sometimes not prescribed, include angiotensin-converting enzyme inhibitors for heart failure and anticoagulants for nonvalvular atrial fibrillation.

Prescribing medications for older adults requires maintaining a balance between using too few and too little, and too many and too much. Frequent follow-up visits, especially if a new drug has been introduced, allow the physician to assess for adverse drug events and possible drug-disease and drug-drug interactions. One recommended strategy is to verify at each patient visit if there is an indication for each drug, if it is effective in this case, if there is any unnecessary duplication with other drugs, and if this is the least expensive drug available compared with others of equal benefit. Before deciding that a medication is a therapeutic failure, the physician should make sure that an adequate dosage has been administered for an appropriate length of time. The goals in using drug therapy are to treat disease, alleviate pain and suffering, and prevent the life-threatening complications of many chronic diseases.

Being successful with these goals requires a balance between benefit and risk to optimize prescribing for the aging population.

12

Overprescription of Antibiotics Has Led to Resistant Bacteria

Linda Bren

Linda Bren is a staff writer for FDA Consumer.

Antibiotics are medications with the capacity to destroy disease-causing bacteria. Antibiotic-resistant bacteria have been appearing since the advent of these so-called miracle drugs fifty years ago, but in the past ten years the number of resistant bacteria has increased. While bacteria can develop resistance naturally, they often become resistant in response to antibiotics that are overused by patients and physicians. Doctors cite a number of reasons for overprescribing these drugs, including pressure from patients who show no signs of bacterial infection. The Food and Drug Administration (FDA) is focusing on two methods for lessening the potential danger of antibiotic resistance: encouraging doctors and their patients to use antibiotics with greater care and caution and promoting the development of newer, stronger antibiotics.

Ever since antibiotics became widely available about 50 years ago, they have been hailed as miracle drugs—magic bullets able to destroy disease-causing bacteria.

But with each passing decade, bacteria that resist not only single, but multiple, antibiotics—making some diseases

Linda Bren, "Battle of the Bugs: Fighting Antibiotic Resistance," *FDA Consumer*, July/August 2002, revised September 2003.

particularly hard to control—have become increasingly widespread. In fact, according to the Centers for Disease Control and Prevention (CDC), virtually all significant bacterial infections in the world are becoming resistant to the antibiotic treatment of choice. For some of us, bacterial resistance could mean more visits to the doctor, a lengthier illness, and possibly more toxic drugs. For others, it could mean death. The CDC estimates that each year, nearly 2 million people in the United States acquire an infection while in a hospital, resulting in 90,000 deaths. More than 70 percent of the bacteria that cause these infections are resistant to at least one of the antibiotics commonly used to treat them.

Antibiotic resistance, also known as antimicrobial resistance, is not a new phenomenon. Just a few years after the first antibiotic, penicillin, became widely used in the late 1940s, penicillin-resistant infections emerged that were caused by the bacterium *Staphylococcus aureus (S. aureus)*. These "staph" infections range from urinary tract infections to bacterial pneumonia. Methicillin, one of the strongest in the arsenal of drugs to treat staph infections, is no longer effective against some strains of *S. aureus*. Vancomycin, which is the most lethal drug against these resistant pathogens, may be in danger of losing its effectiveness; recently, some strains of *S. aureus* that are resistant to vancomycin have been reported.

Bacteria Are Developing Resistance

Although resistant bacteria have been around a long time, the scenario today is different from even just 10 years ago, says Stuart Levy, M.D., president of the Alliance for the Prudent Use of Antibiotics. "The number of bacteria resistant to many different antibiotics has increased, in many cases, tenfold or more. Even new drugs that have been approved are confronting resistance, fortunately in small amounts, but we have to be careful how they're used. If used for extended periods of time, they too risk becoming ineffective early on." ...

The ability of antibiotics to stop an infection depends on killing or halting the growth of harmful bacteria. But some bacteria resist the effects of drugs and multiply and spread.

Some bacteria have developed resistance to antibiotics naturally, long before the development of commercial antibiotics. After testing bacteria found in an arctic glacier and estimated to be over 2,000 years old, scientists found several of them to be resistant against some antibiotics, most likely indicating naturally occurring resistance.

According to the CDC, antibiotic prescribing ... could be reduced by more than 30 percent without adversely affecting patient health.

If they are not naturally resistant, bacteria can become resistant to drugs in a number of ways. They may develop resistance to certain drugs spontaneously through mutation. Mutations are changes that occur in the genetic material, or DNA, of the bacteria. These changes allow the bacteria to fight or inactivate the antibiotic. ...

Preserving Antibiotics' Usefulness

Two main types of germs—bacteria and viruses—cause most infections, according to the CDC. But while antibiotics can kill bacteria, they do not work against viruses—and it is viruses that cause colds, the flu, and most sore throats. In fact, only 15 percent of sore throats are caused by the bacterium *Streptococcus*, which results in strep throat. In addition, it is viruses that cause most sinus infections, coughs, and bronchitis. And fluid in the middle ear, a common occurrence in children, does not usually warrant treatment with antibiotics unless there are other symptoms. ...

Nevertheless, "Every year, tens of millions of prescriptions for antibiotics are written to treat viral illnesses for which these antibiotics offer no benefits," says David Bell, M.D., the

CDC's antimicrobial resistance coordinator. According to the CDC, antibiotic prescribing in outpatient settings could be reduced by more than 30 percent without adversely affecting patient health.

Reasons cited by doctors for overprescribing antibiotics include diagnostic uncertainty, time pressure on physicians, and patient demand. Physicians are pressured by patients to prescribe antibiotics, says Bell. "People don't want to miss work, or they have a sick child who kept the whole family up all night, and they're willing to try anything that might work." It may be easier for the physician pressed for time to write a prescription for an antibiotic than it is to explain why it might be better not to use one.

But by taking an antibiotic, a person may be doubly harmed, according to Bell. First, it offers no benefit for viral infections, and second, it increases the chance of a drug-resistant infection appearing at a later time.

"Antibiotic resistance is not just a problem for doctors and scientists," says Bell. "Everybody needs to help deal with this. An important way that people can help directly is to understand that common illnesses like colds and the flu do not benefit from antibiotics and to not request them to treat these illnesses."

Following the prescription exactly is also important, says Bell. People should not skip doses or stop taking an antibiotic as soon as they feel better; they should complete the full course of the medication. Otherwise, the drug may not kill all the infectious bacteria, allowing the remaining bacteria to possibly become resistant.

Antibiotic Resistance Campaigns

While some antibiotics must be taken for 10 days or more, others are FDA-approved for a shorter course of treatment. Some can be taken for as few as three days. "I would prefer the short course to the long course," says Levy. "Reservoirs of antibiotic resistance are not being stimulated as much. The shorter the course, theoretically, the less chance you'll have resistance emerging, and it gives susceptible strains a better chance to come back."

The FDA published a final rule in February 2003 ... to encourage doctors to prescribe [antibiotics] only when truly necessary.

Another concern to some health experts is the escalating use of antibacterial soaps, detergents, lotions, and other household items. "There has never been evidence that they have a public health benefit," says Levy. "Good soap and water is sufficient in most cases." Antibacterial products should be reserved for the hospital setting, for sick people coming home from the hospital, and for those with compromised immune systems, says Levy.

To decrease both demand and overprescribing, the FDA and the CDC have launched antibiotic resistance campaigns aimed at health-care professionals and the public. A nationwide ad campaign developed by the FDA's Center for Drug Evaluation and Research emphasizes to health-care professionals the prudent use of antibiotics, and offers them an educational brochure to distribute to patients.

The FDA published a final rule in February 2003 that requires specific language on human antibiotic labels to encourage doctors to prescribe them only when truly necessary. The rule also requires a statement in the labeling encouraging doctors to counsel their patients about the proper use of these drugs.

Stimulating Drug Development

The FDA is working to encourage the development of new antibiotics and new classes of antibiotics and other antimicrobials. "We would like to make it attractive for the development of new antibiotics, but we'd like people to use them less and only in the presence of bacterial infection," says [the FDA's Mark] Goldberger. This presents a challenge, he says. "Decreased use may result in sales going down, and drug companies may feel there are better places to put their resources."

Through such incentives as exclusivity rights, the FDA hopes to stimulate new antimicrobial drug development. Exclusivity protects a manufacturer's drug from generic drug competition for a specific length of time.

The FDA has a variety of existing regulatory tools to help developers of antimicrobial drugs. One of these is an accelerated approval process for drugs that treat severely debilitating or life-threatening diseases and for drugs that show meaningful benefit over existing prescription drugs to cure a disease.

The FDA is also investigating other approaches for speeding the antimicrobial approval process. One approach is to reduce the size of the clinical trial program. "We need to streamline the review process without compromising safety and effectiveness," says Goldberger. "One of the things that we are trying to look at now is how we can substitute quality for quantity in clinical studies." It has been difficult to test drugs for resistance in people, says Goldberger. "Although these resistant organisms are a problem, they are still not so common that it is very easy to accumulate patients."

Scientists and health professionals are generally in agreement that a way to decrease antibiotic resistance is through more cautious use of antibiotic drugs and through monitoring outbreaks of drug-resistant infections.

But research is also critical to help understand the various mechanisms that pathogens use to evade drugs. Understanding these mechanisms is important for the design of effective new drugs.

Organizations to Contact

AARP
601 E St. NW
Washington, DC 20049
(888) 687-2277
Web site: www.aarp.org

Formerly the American Association of Retired Persons, AARP is now known by its acronym. A nonprofit, nonpartisan membership organization dedicated to people aged fifty and over, AARP advocates for positive social change and also provides members' benefits. AARP publishes the bimonthly *AARP Bulletin*, the monthly *AARP Magazine*, and a Spanish-language newspaper, *Segunda Juventud*.

Alliance for Aging Research
2021 K St. NW, Suite 305
Washington, DC 20006
(202) 293-2856 • fax: (202) 785-8574
e-mail: info@agingresearch.org
Web site: www.agingresearch.org

The Alliance for Aging Research is the nation's leading advocacy organization with the goal of improving the health and independence of aging Americans. It supports scientific advancement and better access to information about these advances, as a means of empowering aging people. It publishes consumer brochures on topics such as colon cancer, osteoporosis, and arthritis treatments, as well as the quarterly newsletter *Living Longer & Loving It!*

Alliance for the Prudent Use of Antibiotics (APUA)
75 Kneeland St.
Boston, MA 02111-1901
(617) 636-0966 • fax: (617) 636-3999
e-mail: apua@tufts.edu

Web site: www.tufts.edu/med/apua

APUA is an organization whose goal is promoting appropriate use of antibiotics and curbing antibiotic resistance worldwide. It has been raising public awareness about antibiotic resistance since 1981. Its publications include the quarterly *APUA Newsletter*.

American Medical Association (AMA)
515 N. State St.
Chicago, IL 60610
(800) 621-8335
Web site: www.ama-assn.org

The AMA is America's largest physician group. It advocates on issues affecting health care in the United States, including Medicare reform and medical liability reform. It publishes *Journal of the American Medical Association (JAMA)* as well as *AMA Voice* and *American Medical News*, which are both available on the organization's Web site.

American Psychiatric Association
1000 Wilson Blvd., Suite 1825
Arlington, VA 22209-3901
(703) 907-7300
e-mail: apa@psych.org
Web sites: www.psych.org
www.healthyminds.org

The American Psychiatric Association is an organization of physicians specializing in the field of psychiatry. The association is dedicated to providing humane and effective treatment for all people who suffer from mental disorders and works toward a society where quality psychiatric treatment is available and accessible to all who need it. It publishes fact sheets on issues such as confidentiality, managed care, and postpartum depression and *Let's Talk Facts*, brochures on topics such as choosing a psychiatrist and teen suicide.

American Society on Aging
833 Market St., Suite 511
San Francisco, CA 94103
(415) 974-9600 • fax: (415) 974-0300
e-mail: info@asaging.org
Web site: www.asaging.org

Founded in 1954, the American Society on Aging seeks to support and enhance the knowledge and skills of those who improve the quality of life of older adults and their families. It offers educational programming and numerous resources to researchers, practitioners, educators, businesspeople, policy makers, and students. Its publications include the quarterly journal *Generations*, the bimonthly newspaper *Aging Today*, and the e-mail newsletter and online magazine *ASA Connection*.

Center for Drug Evaluation and Research
Food and Drug Administration
5600 Fishers La.
Rockville, MD 20857-0001
(888) 463-6332
Web site: www.fda.gov/cder

The Center for Drug Evaluation and Research, a division of the Food and Drug Administration, ensures the safety and effectiveness of drugs available to the American public. Its publications include the *CDER Handbook* and fact sheets about drugs.

Center for Studying Health System Change
600 Maryland Ave. SW, #550
Washington, DC 20024
(202) 484-5261 • fax: (202) 484-9258
e-mail: hscinfo@hschange.org
Web site: www.hschange.org

The center is a nonpartisan policy research organization that studies the American health-care system in order to inform policy makers. Its publications include issue briefs, community reports, tracking reports, and data bulletins.

Children and Adults with Attention-Deficit/Hyperactivity Disorder (CHADD)

8181 Professional Pl., Suite 150
Landover, MD 20785
(800) 233-4050
Web site: www.chadd.org

CHADD is the nation's leading nonprofit organization devoted to individuals with ADHD. It provides informative materials on the disorder to parents, educators, professionals, media, and the general public. Among its publications are the bimonthly *Attention!* magazine for members, *Where We Stand* position papers, and *What We Know* fact sheets.

Get Smart
Centers for Disease Control and Prevention (CDC)

1600 Clifton Rd.
Atlanta, GA 30333
(404) 639-3534
Web site: www.cdc.gov/drugresistance/community

In 1995 the CDC launched Get Smart, its national campaign to combat antimicrobial resistance by educating the public and advocating for appropriate antibiotic use. It publishes brochures, posters, Q&A sheets, and other educational materials.

National Alliance on Mental Illness (NAMI)

Colonial Place Three, 2107 Wilson Blvd., Suite 300
Arlington, VA 22201-3042
(703) 524-7600 • fax: (703) 524-9094
e-mail: info@nami.org
Web site: www.nami.org

NAMI is America's largest grassroots mental health organization. It is dedicated to improving the lives of persons with serious mental illness and the lives of their families through advocacy, research, support, and education. Its Web site provides educational information about mental illnesses and treatments. It also publishes the quarterly magazine *Advocate* for its members.

National Hospice and Palliative Care Organization (NHPCO)

1700 Diagonal Rd., Suite 625
Alexandria, VA 22314
(703) 837-1500 • fax: (703) 837-1233
e-mail: nhpco_info@nhpco.org
Web site: www.nhpco.org

The NHPCO is a nonprofit organization that represents hospice and palliative care programs and professionals in the United States. It is committed to improving end-of-life care and expanding access to hospice care. Its publications include *NHPCO NewsBriefs*.

Pharmaceutical Research and Manufacturers of America (PhRMA)

1100 Fifteenth St. NW
Washington, DC 20005
(202) 835-3400
Web site: www.phrma.org

PhRMA is an organization representing the pharmaceutical industry. It advocates for the industry, its members, and public policy that supports the development and sale of new medicines. Among its publications are yearly reports on the pharmaceutical industry, several newsletters, including *Rx Minute*, and fact sheets and policy papers.

Physicians Committee for Responsible Medicine (PCRM)

5100 Wisconsin Ave. NW, Suite 400
Washington, DC 20016-4131

(202) 686-2210 • fax: (202) 686-2216
e-mail: pcrm@pcrm.org
Web site: www.pcrm.org

PCRM is a nonprofit organization of both physicians and laypersons founded in 1985. It advocates compassionate and effective health-care practices as well as higher ethical standards in medical research. PCRM publishes the quarterly magazine *Good Medicine*.

Public Citizen Health Research Group
1600 Twentieth St. NW
Washington, DC 20009
(202) 588-1000
e-mail: hrg1@citizen.org
Web site: www.citizen.org/hrg

The Health Research Group is a division of Public Citizen, a consumer watchdog group founded by Ralph Nader. The Health Research Group promotes changes in health-care policy and provides oversight of medical treatment, including drugs, medical devices, doctors, and hospitals. It does not accept funds from corporations, professional associations, or government agencies. Its publications include the monthly *Health Letter*. It also maintains a consumer-education Web site, www.worstpills.org

Bibliography

Books

Marcia Angell	*The Truth About the Drug Companies: How They Deceive Us and What to Do About It.* New York: Random House, 2004.
Jerry Avorn	*Powerful Medicines: The Benefits, Risks, and Costs of Prescription Drugs.* New York: Knopf, 2004.
Peter R. Breggin	*The Antidepressant Fact Book: What Your Doctor Won't Tell You About Prozac, Zoloft, Paxil, Celexa, and Luvox.* New York: Perseus, 2001.
Peter R. Breggin	*The Ritalin Fact Book: What Your Doctor Won't Tell You.* New York: Perseus, 2002.
Alan Cassels and Ray Moynihan	*Selling Sickness: How the World's Biggest Pharmaceutical Companies Are Turning Us All into Patients.* New York: Nation, 2005.
Merrill Goozner	*The $800 Million Pill: The Truth Behind the Cost of New Drugs.* Berkeley and Los Angeles: University of California Press, 2004.
Katharine Greider	*The Big Fix: How the Pharmaceutical Industry Rips Off American Consumers.* New York: PublicAffairs, 2003.

David Healy

Let Them Eat Prozac: The Unhealthy Relationship Between the Pharmaceutical Industry and Depression. New York: New York University Press, 2004.

Jerome P. Kassirer

On The Take: How Medicine's Complicity with Big Business Can Endanger Your Health. Oxford: Oxford University Press, 2004.

Fred Leavitt

The REAL Drug Abusers. Lanham, MD: Rowman & Littlefield, 2003.

Stuart Levy

The Antibiotic Paradox. New York: Perseus, 2001.

Peter Lurie, Larry D. Sasich, and Sidney M. Wolfe

Worst Pills, Best Pills: A Consumer's Guide to Avoiding Drug-Induced Death or Illness. New York: Pocket Books, 2005.

Rick Ng

Drugs: From Discovery to Approval. Hoboken, NJ: Wiley-Liss, 2004.

Jamie Reidy

Hard Sell: The Evolution of a Viagra Salesman. Kansas City, MO: Andrews McMeel, 2005.

Periodicals

Doug Bandow

"Demonizing Those Who Cure Us," *National Review Online*, July 24, 2003.

Sara Corbett

"The Asthma Trap," *Mother Jones*, March/April 2005.

Carol Marie Cropper

"The Inside Dope on Drugs," *Business Week*, December 13, 2004.

Jeff Donn   "Experts Say Americans Are
                       Overmedicating," Associated Press,
                       April 18, 2005.

Glenn Ellis   "Overuse of Antibiotics Can Make
                       You Sicker," *Philadelphia Tribune*,
                       September 6, 2005.

Yves Engler   "The Pharmaceutical Drive to Drug,"
                       Humanist, May/June 2003.

Michael Fumento   "Trick Question—a Liberal 'Hoax'
                       Turns Out to Be True," *New Republic*,
                       February 3, 2003.

Howard Gleckman   "Seniors' Big Drug Problem:
                       Misusing Medications Is a Leading
                       Cause of Death Among the Elderly,"
                       Business Week, December 22, 2003.

Erica Goode   "Antidepressants Lift Clouds, but
                       Lose 'Miracle Drug' Label," *New York
                       Times*, June 30, 2002.

Christine Gorman   "A Painful Mistake," *Time*, October
                       11, 2004.

Bernadine Healy   "What Is a 'Safe Drug'?" *U.S. News &
                       World Report*, December 13, 2004.

Katherine Hobson   "A Prescription for Poverty," *U.S.
                       News & World Report*, June 3, 2002.

Jeffrey Kluger   "Medicating Young Minds," *Time*,
                       November 3, 2003.

Ivan Oransky   "Antibiotic Overuse Can Silence
                       Medicine's Big Guns," *USA Today*,
                       final edition, November 15, 2001.

Andrew Solomon   "A Bitter Pill," *New York Times*, late
                       edition, March 29, 2004.

Jennifer Steinhauer   "That Prescription Drug Trap," *New York Times*, late edition/East Coast, May 20, 2001.

Steve Sternberg   "Chronic Pain: The Enemy Within," *USA Today*, final edition, May 9, 2005.

Index